MR. M

"I'm not sure what

crazy story that might somehow matter."

"Nothing is ever too crazy for this asylum you call a town," Victor said. "Spill it."

I told him what Susan told me about Matilda Biggs and Spellman.

A smirk emerged on Victor's face. "Now we're getting somewhere."

I smashed a mosquito lurking by my ankle, ready to strike. "Hey, I'm telling you, this Susan woman might be just as nuts as the rest of them. She could've made it up on the spot for all I know," I said.

"Easy enough to find out," he said, pushing himself off the steps and adjusting his hat. "I'll talk to Mama Biggs and work out the financials. She wants to ante up, we can visit this little meeting tomorrow night and see what shakes out."

I glanced up at the window, then back at him. "I promised Julianne I'd stay out of this one."

"You mean like every other case we take?"

I paused. "Yes."

He grinned as his little legs took him to his car. "So figure out a way to start apologizing to her."

More Stay at Home Dad Mysteries
by Jeffrey Allen

STAY AT HOME DEAD

POPPED OFF

FATHER KNOWS DEATH

Published by Kensington Publishing Corp.

Father Knows Death

Jeffrey Allen

KENSINGTON PUBLISHING CORP.
http://www.kensingtonbooks.com

KENSINGTON BOOKS are published by

Kensington Publishing Corp.
119 West 40th Street
New York, NY 10018

All Kensington Titles, Imprints, and Distributed Lines are available at special quantity discounts for bulk purchases for sales promotions, premiums, fund-raising, and educational or institutional use.

Special book excerpts or customized printings can also be created to fit specific needs. For details, write or phone the office of the Kensington special sales manager: Kensington Publishing Corp., 119 West 40th Street, New York, NY 10018, attn: Special Sales Department, Phone: 1-800-221-2647.

Kensington and the K logo Reg. U.S. Pat & TM Off.

ISBN-13: 978-0-7582-6691-0
ISBN-10: 0-7582-6691-X

First Kensington Mass Market Edition: June 2013

eISBN-13: 978-0-7582-8903-2
eISBN-10: 0-7582-8903-0

First Kensington Electronic Edition: June 2013

10 9 8 7 6 5 4 3 2 1

Printed in the United States of America

Father Knows Death

1

George Spellman's lifeless face gazed at me amid the packages of frozen bratwursts.

I stared at him for a moment and then closed the freezer door. Not because I was shocked or horrified at finding a dead body. I closed it because I realized I wasn't fazed by finding a dead man stuffed inside a freezer. I wondered if I should just stop opening things.

It was late April and I was working the grill at the Carriveau County Fair. Rose Petal was in the heart of Carriveau County and our fair was an anomaly. Because Texas summers were so hot, our fair was held every April. All of the towns in the county shut down, schools were closed, and everyone spent the entire week at the fair. It was like an extra week of spring break, but with carnival rides, farm animals, and lots of fried food. Monday and Tuesday were spent setting up, cleaning out the barns, getting the animals delivered and letting the ride operators get their rides set up. Wednesday, everyone rolled in. It had been that way, on that schedule, for as long as anyone could remember.

Carly had joined our local 4-H chapter last year because she liked the furry little animals, and one of their big fund-raisers was working the food stand during the fair. The summer temperatures had moved in early this year, however, and there was nothing quite like working an outdoor grill in hundred-degree heat. So much for avoiding the heat.

"I think we're gonna need some more burgers and dogs for the grill, Deuce," Pete Boodle said, wiping his brow with a red bandanna. "Some brats, too. Lunch rush is gonna be any minute."

The large grill was littered with thin hamburger patties, hot dogs, and a few bratwursts. They were probably seasoned with a bit of Pete's sweat.

"There's a big freezer in the back," he said, pointing toward the kitchen. "We use it for extra storage. Should be a bunch in there."

"How many should I grab?" I asked.

"As many as you can carry," he said, chuckling. "It's gonna be a madhouse in about five minutes."

We'd been working nonstop since our four-hour shift began and I found it hard to believe it could get any busier. I could think of about fifty other things I would've rather been doing on a Wednesday afternoon than basting myself over a dirty grill at our county fair. But there's one thing you learn as a parent: when your kid signs up for something, you're signing up for it, too.

"All right," I told Pete. "Be back in a minute."

"Grab us some drinks, too." He flipped the already overdone patties again. "So we don't die out here."

I waved at him and stepped into the food stand kitchen, which was nothing more than a saunalike shack that disguised itself as a fast-food restaurant for one week a year. There was a covered eating area for about a hundred people, front and back counters, a giant indoor grill and fryer, some sinks, and a bunch of refrigerators.

Oh, and about fifty people squeezed into the kitchen trying to serve the fairgoers.

Voices screamed and yelled about cheese and drinks and burgers and buns as people who had no business serving and preparing food attempted to do just that.

A pink-faced Carly squeezed by me, carrying two bottles of water. "Hey, Daddy."

"What's up, kid?"

"I'm getting water," she shouted. "For some people!"

Her oversize green 4-H shirt hung nearly to her knees and her hair was hidden beneath a bright yellow bandanna. She was nearly six years old and starting to assert her independence already.

"Good for you, kiddo."

She scurried past me and snaked her way through the group of workers out to the front counter to deliver her water.

Julianne was perched on a tall stool, her gloved hands submerged in a deep sink, washing orange and green plastic trays.

I walked over and kissed her sweaty cheek. "You should probably be at home."

She spun on the stool to look at me. Her green T-shirt was riding up over her enormous stomach.

"Why?" she asked, setting down a tray. "Because its seven hundred degrees in here and I'm like fourteen months pregnant?"

"Yes. Exactly."

"I'm tough."

I touched her very round belly. "I know that. I'm just hoping the new kid likes the heat."

"They won't have a choice. We live in Texas, Deuce."

"Doesn't mean you need to boil them in your stomach."

"I'm hoping that will encourage it to get the hell out of my body," she said.

Julianne was a week past her due date and looked ready to pop. Because I enjoyed my health, I didn't say that out loud. But she'd been carrying around a baby for ten months now and she was ready to bond with it in person. We all were.

"I'm going to get meat" I said.

"Oh, great. I'll just stay here and wash trays and be enormous."

"And beautiful."

"Ha. Good one, Sausage Boy."

I kissed her again. "I love you."

"And I want this kid out of me and I swear to God, I'll have it right in this disgusting kitchen if I need to," she said, spinning back on the stool. "Oh, and I love you, too."

Pregnant women are funny.

I wound my way through the back of the kitchen, my thoughts focused on babies instead of sausages. I was excited that the baby was going to be here any day. Carly was, too. We were all ready to meet the newest member of the Winters family. We had no idea whether it was a boy or a girl. Julianne insisted on not knowing. I'd protested greatly. And it didn't matter even a little, though it was still a bit weird to keep calling the baby "it."

"Babies should be a surprise," she'd said. "Like presents on Christmas. Plus, it's in *my* uterus so I get to decide."

Which was a hard point to argue with.

I liked seeing her pregnant. I didn't like seeing her miserable, though, and with the early heat, I knew she had to be pretty uncomfortable. But I did have this fear that her water was going to break right in the middle of the dinner rush and that would be some sort of health code violation.

And so I was thinking about babies and having to rush to the hospital when I opened the freezer and saw George Spellman's dead face amongst the bratwursts.

And after thinking that I needed to stop opening things, my next thought was that a dead body in the freezer was probably a far worse health code violation than having a baby in the kitchen.

2

"Well, this isn't good," Matilda Biggs said, shaking her head.

The technicians were loading the body into the back of the ambulance and the police had formed a barricade around the back of the food stand. Matilda, a member of the fair board, was concerned. More than concerned. Mortified.

"No, it isn't," I agreed.

She swallowed hard. "This is awful. Awful." Tears glistened in her eyes. "This is really going to reflect poorly on the fair," she said. "Could drive down revenue."

"Uh, yeah," I said. I was less concerned about revenue than I was for George's family and friends.

She paced back and forth, wringing her hands. "I mean, Rusty Cow plays tonight," she said, staring at me. "We're expecting a big crowd. Huge. It wouldn't be good if we had to cancel that."

It felt like there was something more that she was worried about, but I couldn't put my finger on it. I wasn't really buying that her main concern was attendance at a concert for a crappy local band. I didn't know Matilda well, but I knew of her. She was hard not to know of because she was hard to miss.

She weighed nearly four hundred pounds.

And that wasn't one of those exaggerated statements about someone carrying a few extra pounds. She was one of the biggest women I'd ever seen. She was just short of six feet and seemingly almost as wide, with rolls of fat billowing from every part of her body. I'd only ever seen her wearing black sweats and some sort of stretched-out T-shirt, as I assumed she wasn't able to find anything else to fit her enormous body. Her stringy black hair was thinning on top and stuck to the sides of her head with sweat. She was never more than a few feet away from her golf cart, as that was the only way she was able to make it around the fairgrounds.

She wiped at her eyes, pulled a walkie-talkie from her hip, and punched a button. "Mama, this is Matilda. You copy? Over."

Five seconds later, the walkie-talkie crackled.

"This is Mama. Roger that, I copy. Over."

Mama was not code for some motherly figure in Matilda's life. Mama was Mama. Matilda's mother. Who worked right alongside her on the fair board. I didn't know the specifics, but I was pretty sure the entire fair board was somehow related to each other.

"We're gonna need a new freezer," Matilda said. "The police are telling me we can't use this one, on account of Deuce Winters finding George Spellman in it. George is gone." She paused. "Over."

The Rose Petal police had, in fact, cordoned off the large freezer with yellow crime scene tape.

"Roger. I'm already on it," Mama said through the walkie-talkie. "I've got another one on the way. Should be there in about fifteen minutes. Over."

Matilda nodded. "Ten-four." She stuck the radio back on her hip. "I gotta make some calls." She glanced at the back of the ambulance for a long moment. "Make sure we got more sausages coming."

She waddled over to the golf cart, wedged herself in behind the steering wheel, and took off, spraying dirt and weeds behind her.

Carly and Julianne made their way around the food stand building to me. Carly surveyed the scene, trying to take everything in. I resisted the urge to pull down the bandanna from her hair to cover her eyes.

Julianne just raised her eyebrows. "Well, this is interesting. You already talk to the police?"

"Yeah. Took all of five minutes. I didn't do anything other than open the freezer door."

"Maybe this time you won't be a suspect."

I narrowed my eyes. "Very funny."

She shrugged. "You sort of have a way of falling into these things."

It was hard to deny that, as much as I might've liked to. My part-time private investigating gig only existed because I kept finding myself embroiled in the criminal activity in Rose Petal. Julianne had made several subtle suggestions that, with a new baby on the way, maybe I might want to curtail my activity in that arena. I didn't disagree.

But it seemed that trouble was still finding me, no matter how much I tried to avoid it.

As I contemplated that, Susan Blamunski hustled our way.

"Oh, good Lord," Julianne whispered. "Red alert. Crazy woman dead ahead."

Susan's face was a mask of concern.

And of heavy eye makeup.

Her large mane of dark hair was teased up and hair-sprayed to death, so much so that I was sure it would've taken a missile to penetrate its exterior. Her 4-H T-shirt was expertly tied at the hip, just above her denim capris. Her sparkly silver sandals seemed a poor choice for a day at the fair, but she'd probably chosen them to match the sparkly silver polish on her toes.

"Deuce," she said, grabbing me by the elbow. "What is going *on*?"

I tried to casually shake free from the grasp of our local 4-H leader, but failed. "I'm not completely sure."

"I heard they found a dead body," she said,

her decorated eyes widening. She glanced at Julianne and seemed to just notice that she was there. "Oh, hello, Julianne. So nice to see you. We rarely get the opportunity to see you at 4-H events."

The corners of Julianne's mouth twitched. I could see the muscles in her face tense as she held back a retort. She wasn't one to bite her tongue, but for the sake of our daughter, she said, "Hello, Susan."

"So nice that your entire family could work the fair," Susan said to me. "Finally."

"We worked it last year," Julianne said through gritted teeth.

"Did you?" Susan asked, pursing her perfectly glossed lips. "I don't recall. Seems like we see you so . . . infrequently."

If Julianne had had access to a hammer, I was pretty sure she would've used it on Susan's skull at that moment. The fact that Julianne was in the process of establishing her own law practice after leaving her firm earlier in the year meant she was having to put in some serious hours before the baby was born.

But Susan's digs about our family were nothing we hadn't heard before. Our nontraditional family was still a novelty in Rose Petal. People couldn't seem to get used to the role reversal we'd chosen in our home. It worked just fine for us, but there was no doubt that we were the topic of much conversation throughout town.

Julianne took Carly's hand. "Come on, baby.

Let's go check out the bunnies. Before they have another dead body to deal with."

If Susan picked up on the fact that she was the potential other body, she didn't show it.

"When is she due?" she asked.

"Supposed to be a week ago," I said. "Any day now."

"That explains her size," she murmured. She tugged on her own green shirt, smoothing it over her flat stomach. "I don't think I gained more than nine pounds with either of my kids. But I have a terrific metabolism to begin with, so it's actually hard for me to gain weight." She smiled at me. "But you've probably noticed that."

"Uh, sure."

She refocused on the activity around us. "So, I heard they found some man in the freezer."

"Yeah."

"And was it really George? George Spellman?"

I nodded.

"And you . . . you found him?"

"Yeah."

She squeezed my elbow. "How terrible! Why was he in there?"

"Uh, I don't know. I just found him."

The concern in her eyes now outweighed her makeup. "That is terrible." She was silent for a minute, an expensively manicured fingernail in between her lips. "This isn't going to be good. Did they say anything about the food stand?"

"Not yet." I watched her. Like Matilda had been, it seemed like Susan was concerned, but not necessarily because someone had died.

Susan appeared to be worried about something more than the food stand, too. But I didn't know about what.

"We get nearly all of our funding from this week at the fair," she said. "Without it, we won't have any money for activities. For anything."

That was the truth. The food stand was the major fund-raiser each year for our local 4-H. Nothing else brought in an even comparable amount of money. The entire year was built around one week of earnings.

"I'm sure the police will be done soon." I wasn't sure at all, but it seemed like a good way to placate her.

Susan looked around the area. "And didn't I see Matilda over here earlier?"

"Yeah, she was here," I said. "But I think she went to find out about the new freezer or something."

Susan's lips tightened together. "Well, that's interesting."

"What? That she went to find a new freezer?"

"No, no," Susan said, lowering her voice. She looked up at me like she was about to share the most earth-shattering secret in the world with me. "I heard something . . . interesting."

"You keep using that word."

She glanced around me before settling her eyes on mine. "I heard that she was having an affair with George."

3

I wasn't sure I'd heard correctly. "Matilda??"

Susan nodded her head, her hairspray-drenched curls bobbing obediently. "Yes. She and George. Together. Everyone is talking about it."

I was pretty sure the only person talking about it was Susan. And if other people were talking about it, it was because of her.

"Hmm. That is . . . interesting."

She waited for me to ask questions. I didn't.

"Don't you want to know what's going on?" she asked. "Maybe something happened between them. Maybe *she* was the one who put him in the freezer. I thought you were an 'investigator.'"

"I am. But I'm not working this case." Or any case at the moment, which was pretty much fine with me.

"You might want to, after you hear about Matilda."

She wasn't gonna stop, so I gave in. "Fine. What makes you think they were having an affair?"

Susan pulled me away from the food stand, toward the arts and crafts building. I wasn't sure why. It wasn't as if people were crowding around, gawking at the crime scene. George's body had been removed and most of the police cars were gone. One car was still parked next to the building, a dark blue unmarked sedan. The detective working the case.

Susan stopped just short of the entrance to the arts and crafts building and pulled me next to the wall.

"I saw them," she whispered. "*Together.*"

I flinched. I wasn't so sure I wanted more details about four-hundred-pound Matilda and her supposed lover. There were some things the mind refused to forget.

"At Texas Roadhouse," she continued, and I breathed a sigh of relief.

"You saw them at dinner?" I said. "I'm sure they were friends, Susan. George was the groundskeeper here for years. They could've been discussing fair stuff."

George Spellman had operated a small lawn service business in Rose Petal. He also moonlighted as the groundskeeper at the Carriveau County fairgrounds during the summer.

Susan shook her head. "No. This was not a

business dinner. I promise you. They weren't discussing grass or repairs or whatever else it was he did around here."

I'll admit, I was becoming a bit more curious. "How do you know? And I thought you said you *heard* they were having an affair? Who told you that?"

"Oh, everyone is talking, trust me," she said, her fingernails digging into my forearm. "But there were tears. She was crying. She was clutching his arm. I think . . . I think he might have been leaving her. Ending the relationship."

This was a woman who watched far too many soap operas.

"You know, people might say the same thing about me and you," I said.

Her mouth formed a perfect O. "Oh?"

I glanced at my arm. "You just pulled me away from a crowd. You're whispering into my ear. Clutching my arm. . . ."

She dropped my arm like it was a stick crawling with fire ants.

"Deuce Winters! I am insulted!" She stepped away, the picture of indignation. "That is not what this is about!"

"Just sayin'." I tried not to laugh. "Look, I gotta go find my wife. Make sure she doesn't hear any rumors about me and you."

I briefly turned back to see Susan glaring after me as I walked away.

Julianne and Carly were in the animal barn along with a sea of other fairgoers. It wasn't air-conditioned, but there were fans circulating the hot air, at least giving the impression that people were being cooled off.

"Is the viper gone?" Julianne sat perched on a tiny chair, her stomach ballooning in front of her. I wasn't sure if she'd be able to get up.

"Yeah, she's gone."

"Daddy, look at this bunny!" Carly sat across from Julianne, the biggest rabbit I'd ever seen huddled in her lap.

"Are you sure that isn't a bear?" I asked. I stroked the rabbit's silky ears.

"I want him," she told me. "He's for sale. The sign on the cage says so. He's only ten dollars!"

"And he probably eats ten dollars' worth of food a day," I said.

"Daddy," Carly said, scolding me. "He's not *that* big." She stood to return the rabbit to its cage. It struggled and scratched the air as she hoisted it up on her shoulder. An older 4-H'er, a girl I didn't know, lurked by the baby pigs.

"Hey," I said, motioning to the girl. "Any chance you can help her get this bunny back in its cage?"

The girl tugged nervously at her braid. "Uh, I don't work with the rabbits."

"Excuse me?"

She cringed, her eyes wide. "They . . . uh . . . they kinda scare me."

"But you're working in the animal barn."

"My mom signed me up. I didn't want to work in here."

I shook my head and rolled my eyes and scooped the massive rabbit from Carly's arms.

Its claws dug into my arms as I struggled with the latch on the cage. I could hear Julianne stifle a giggle as I crammed the bunny back into its cage.

"Wow. What a rabbit wrangler you are," she said.

I glared at her. "You have no idea."

"So, what else did Susan have to say?" Julianne asked.

I stood behind her and rubbed her shoulders. "The usual. Just some rumors about the dead guy."

"What kind of rumors?"

"That he and Matilda Biggs were having an affair."

Julianne whipped her head around to look at me. "Are you serious?"

"Serious that she said that? Yes. Serious that he was? Good God, I hope not. But she seemed . . . off."

"What do you mean?"

"I'm not sure," I said. "Something just didn't seem right. She was upset about the death and about the food stand being messed up, but there was something I couldn't put my finger on. And it was the same thing with Matilda. They were worried about things other than the fact that someone was murdered."

"Deuce." Her voice was filled with warning.

"What?" I dug my fingers into the soft flesh of her shoulders and kneaded gently.

"Do not get involved in this."

"I don't intend to."

"That's not good enough."

She pushed on the seat of the chair, trying to heave herself to a standing position. I grabbed her under the shoulders and helped.

"I mean it," she said, her eyes narrowed. "I am a hundred weeks pregnant. I am about to have a baby. I have a legal practice that needs all of my time and then some. *Do not get involved.*"

I held her to me. "Okay, okay." I kissed the top of her head.

She pushed me away. "Promise me."

"I promise."

"I will kill both you and Victor," she said. "And that's not a euphemism for just being irritated and slapping you upside the head or something. I will honestly kill you both and find a way to get rid of the bodies so that no one will know I did it. I won't use a freezer. I will dig deep, deep graves way out in the country and no one will ever find either of you."

"You really need to have this baby," I said. "You make far fewer death threats when there isn't a child inside you."

She stepped back and placed her hands on her hips. "If someone told me that killing you would get this baby out of me, I'd truly start looking for bullets. It would be hard raising two kids as a single parent. But right now, I'm willing to give it a shot to get this thing out of me."

Ah, motherhood.

4

Julianne took Carly over to the games and rides on the midway and I wandered back to the food stand just in time to see a large, yellow rental truck backing up toward the building. A toothpick-thin guy in a long red wig with horns poking from it and aviator shades guided the truck backward. A cigarette dangled from his lips as he waved a lazy hand at the building, then held it up to signal the truck to stop.

The driver's door swung open and a woman in her seventies hopped out. A tight Afro of gray curls sat on top of her head and thick, black, cat-eye-shaped glasses framed big brown eyes. She wore jeans with an elastic waist along with a Carriveau County Fair T-shirt and white running shoes.

She scowled at the guy in the red wig. "Dang it, Bruce! Get outta the way!"

A befuddled Bruce held his hands out, wondering exactly what he was in the way of. She pushed past him and unlocked the latch on the back of the truck, sending the door up on its tracks. "Now get this out of here, pronto!"

Bruce's shoulders slumped and he pulled out the ramp in the truck. "Yes, Mama."

Mama yanked her walkie-talkie from her hip and muttered into it. She glanced around waiting for a reply when she spotted me and headed in my direction.

"I been wantin' to meet you," she said, squinting at me. "You're the Winters boy, aren't you?"

Boy? "I'm Deuce, yes."

She held out a bony hand. "I'm Mama Biggs. Chairwoman of the fair board. I run the show around here. Your daddy used to work for the bank, right?"

So this was Matilda's mother. And that made Bruce Matilda's brother. I looked at the thin guy in the red wig and couldn't believe two people of such opposite builds could come from the same gene pool. I shook her hand and it was stronger than I expected. "Pleasure. And, yes, he did."

"That's what I thought." She gestured at the truck. "New freezer. On account of George bein' dead in the other one."

"Right."

Bruce backed up slowly with the freezer up on a dolly. It was identical to the other—stainless steel, upright, double doors with a massive handle—and could hold a ton of meat, along with the body of an adult male.

"Now that all that yellow tape is gone, we

can get back to business," Mama said. She eyed me. "Matilda said you were the one that found him."

"That's right."

"I ain't never seen a dead body before," she said. "Was he tough to get outta the freezer?"

"Uh, I didn't try to take him out. Generally, you don't want to disturb the victim before the authorities get to the scene."

The walkie-talkie crackled and someone said something about mini-donuts.

Mama rolled her eyes and held the walkie-talkie up to her mouth. "You tell Eugene that Mama says he either keeps the mini-donut shack open until midnight or I'll come push him in the deep fryer myself."

"Roger that, Mama," the voice said.

She shook her head. "Every year, that dummy wants to close up early. I need a new donut guy." She eyed me. "You do donuts?"

"Make them? No. I just eat them."

"Shame," she said, pulling up on her jeans. "All right, listen. You're one of them private detectives, right?"

"Yes, but . . ."

"And you got that midget as a partner? The bald one that sorta freaks everyone out?"

"Yes, but . . ."

"All right, then," she said as if I wasn't even there. "I'm gonna need you to figure out what happened with George. But you're gonna need to keep it quiet. You report only to me. I don't want no jabberin' about it to anyone."

Bruce was struggling under the weight of the freezer, his steps wobbly and unsure as he backed down the ramp.

"Bruce, I swear to the good Lord," she yelled. "If you drop my new freezer, yours'll be the next dead body they find! And they won't have to look for it in a freezer!"

"Yes, Mama," he groaned as he struggled to get it off the ramp.

"Now, I don't know what you charge," Mama said to me. "But the fair board will be happy to pay a reasonable fee. Nothing ridiculous and if you try to scam me, I'll find out and then you'll be in for it."

"Ma'am, I can't . . . ," I said.

"It's Mama, not ma'am," she barked at me. "Ma'am was my grandmother. So you just figure out what happened to old George and you let me know."

"I think the police are handling it."

She rolled her eyes again. "Oh, well, isn't that peachy? We oughta know something right around *never*, then, right? Those clowns couldn't find a hot dog if you gave 'em the bun and the ketchup!"

Bruce finally made it off the ramp and Mama stomped over to it, picked it up, and slid it back into the base of the truck. She reached up and pulled the cord on the truck door and slammed it down, locking up the hitch.

She pointed at me as she yanked open the driver's door. "Only me, Deuce Winters. You don't talk to no one else. Not that dim-witted son of mine, Bruce, not Matilda, not another soul." She turned on the engine and the truck roared to life. She scowled at me. "You hear me?"

Mama Biggs was already pulling away before I could even try to answer.

5

I stepped over to where Bruce was struggling with the freezer and helped him balance it on the dolly before he was squashed beneath it.

"Thanks, man," he said, the cigarette bobbing in his mouth. "This sucker's heavy."

I helped him maneuver it so that it was up against the back wall of the food stand's kitchen. We lowered it down easily and Bruce slipped the dolly out from under it, wiping streams of sweat off his face.

"Guess that's as good a place as any," he said, staring at it.

"Good enough," I said. "As long as the cord reaches the outlet, we can get to it right there."

"You workin' in there today?" he asked.

"Yeah."

"Score me a hot dog or somethin'?"

"We don't get free food. Sorry."

He frowned and I got the distinct impression he thought I was an idiot.

"Can I ask why you're wearing a wig?" I asked.

He grinned, exposing yellowed teeth. "It's tradition."

"Tradition?"

"Every year, I wear it," he explained. "I had too many beers one year and put it on and wore it. Just took off. It's kinda become a thing. Plus, everyone knows who I am. Kinda hard to miss it."

"I'll say. Are you on the fair board, too?"

He nodded. "Yep." He leaned against the freezer. "That's why I'm doing all the heavy lifting." He dissolved into laughter at his own joke.

"You know George?" I asked.

His laughter died out and he stared at me. "Why?"

"Just asking."

"You heard something?"

"No, I was just curious."

"Hmm. Right." He shrugged. "Sure I knew him. Everyone knew him. He was always around here." His mouth twitched. "But we weren't like buddies or anything, all right? I mean, like, I'd wave at him and say what's up, but not like we went drinkin' together or anything like that." He shook his head.

I started to respond, but he wasn't finished.

"So maybe I didn't really know him. I shouldn't

say that. I was *aware* of him. Yeah. That sounds better."

I was almost sorry I'd asked the question. "Okay. Got it."

"You hear anything different from anyone, you correct them, all right?" he asked, craning his neck at me.

"Sure. Yeah." What an odd request, I thought.

He seemed satisfied with that answer. "All right, then. I'm gonna go get me a beer over at the garden. Board members drink free *over there.*" He grinned. "I'd invite ya, but I guess you gotta get back to cooking hamburgers or something."

I nodded and headed for the stand. Anything was better than spending another moment talking to Bruce.

Leon Cotter was standing near the back of the stand, chewing on a toothpick and adjusting his Rose Petal Sheriff's Department hat on his flat, wide head.

He nodded at me. "Deuce."

"Sheriff," I said. "Busy morning, eh?"

The toothpick shifted from the left side of his mouth to the right. "Could say that."

Leon had just stepped into the sheriff's role in town and no one really knew how to take him. He was quiet and tended to keep to himself. Tall and lanky with a ruddy complexion, he was completely bald beneath the hat. He wasn't seen out and about very often and, given that Rose Petal didn't have a whole lot of crime, that was okay.

"You thinking about looking into Mr. Spellman's death?" he asked, casting a sideways glance at me.

"I don't think so, no," I said, unsure of how to answer after my meet-up with Mama Biggs.

"Good," he said, nodding. "We probably won't get the ball rolling on this until the fair ends."

"Really?"

"We don't want anything getting in the way of the fair," he said. "It'll be fine. He'll still be dead."

"But don't you think letting the investigation sit still might put you at a disadvantage?" I asked. "I'd think you'd want to act quickly."

"Which is why I'm the sheriff and you're not," he said, half a grin settling on his mouth. "This fair is the most important thing in town. We'll preserve evidence. We'll begin the preliminaries. But the biggest crime would be letting something like this overshadow the entire fair week."

The fair might have brought in a lot of money for Rose Petal and community organizations, but I couldn't have disagreed more. Letting a crime investigation sit idle seemed criminal in and of itself. If Victor had taught me anything, it was that once you found a trail of evidence, you didn't let it grow cold. Letting George Spellman's death go unlooked at for several days almost assured that the trail wouldn't just go cold. It would ice over.

"So if you do decide to do some of your own investigating or whatever it is you and that short fella do, I'd appreciate it if you two wait until the fair is over," he said. He tipped his hat in my direction. "And I'd be mighty appreciative if I didn't have to tell you a second time."

6

The stand was busier than before the discovery of George's body, a combination of hungry people and curious onlookers. Pete and I couldn't keep enough meat on the grill, as the orders came fast and furious. When our relief showed up, I had to double-check my watch to make sure the four-hour shift was over.

"Well, that may have been the most exciting food-stand shift ever," Pete said, collapsing on a wooden bench outside the stand. "My goodness."

"You can say that again," I said, sitting down next to him and wiping down my forehead with a paper towel.

The fair was in full swing now. The grounds were overrun with fairgoers, most clutching mammoth-size lemonades or waving cardboard fans in their pitiful attempt to escape the heat. Lines for the Tilt-A-Whirl and Kamikaze snaked sideways, kids whining as they waited their turn to defy death on the rickety rides.

"Not often we lose an hour to a corpse and still do more business than normal," he said, a sly grin on his face.

"I can't believe they're letting us keep it open."

He raised a sweaty eyebrow. "Really? Not me. With all the stuff that goes on around here at the fair, nothing surprises me anymore."

I shrank back as a woman carrying a toddler with a dripping ice cream cone passed by. "That right?"

He nodded. "Yep. Nothing stops the fair."

"Clearly."

Pete chuckled. "Right? You'd think something like this might've put a dent in the day. But if they'd tried to shut us down, she would've come out guns blazing."

"She? Mama?"

He nodded again. "Oh, yeah. Mama Biggs and her entire crew."

"Crew?"

"Matilda. Bruce." He waved a hand absently in the air. "Woody and Wendy. Probably others I don't even know about. That seems like one family tree with a lot of goofy branches."

"Who are they?"

"They're actually in charge of all the fair food," he said. "They're on the fair board, too. It's like a clan or something. Or maybe *gang* is a better word for them. I'm not sure what the best word to describe them is." He stretched out his legs and rubbed his knees. "But I didn't for a second think the police would shut down the food stand. Pretty sure Mama's got some under-the-table deal with them."

"Are Wendy and Woody related to Mama, too?" I said. "And, just so you know, I can't believe we're grown men referring to a grown woman as Mama."

He laughed. "Me, either. But I don't even know her real name. I'm not sure if Woody and Wendy are related to Mama. I don't think so. That might be a little too overt to make every member of her family a board member, even for Mama. Woody and Wendy are married, but you wouldn't know it. They fight like cats and dogs most of the time. Woody should be here any minute." Pete chuckled again. "You can't miss him."

It amazed me that even after living in Rose Petal my entire life, there were still people I didn't know. The town felt so small and so insular that I was always surprised when I heard a name or saw a face that I didn't recognize. I'd known about the fair board as a group for years, but it wasn't until I'd gotten roped into helping with 4-H that I'd learned any of their names.

"And you didn't hear it from me, but there have been lots of whispers about all of them," Pete said.

"Whispers?"

He leaned forward. "None of them have real jobs. All they do is the fair." He raised an eyebrow. "And the board positions are all volunteer."

"None of them are paid?"

"Think Mama might get some sort of nominal stipend for being the chairwoman, but other than that?" Pete shook his head. "They're all unpaid volunteer positions."

I leaned back and watched a stream of people walk by on their way to the free stage and wondered what show might be drawing such a crowd.

"So where are they getting their money?"

Pete sighed. "Midway. Food stands. Ticket booths. You name it." He winked at me. "But, remember. That's just whispers."

Skimming from a county fair was probably more common than I knew. But I didn't like the idea that they might be stealing from local organizations that depended on fair revenue to survive. Like Carly's 4-H group.

"No one's called them on it?" I asked. "Checked out their financials?"

Pete smiled. "You should really come to a fair board meeting. I think you'd enjoy it."

"Why's that?"

The smile stayed on his face. "There's one tomorrow night. They always have one during the week of the fair. Just come and see for yourself."

I made a mental note to try and check it out.

"And if you wondered why the sun just disappeared," Pete said, his smile changing from mischievous to amused, "here comes Woody."

7

As a former football player, I had been around lots of large men, but I wasn't sure I'd ever seen anyone the size of Woody.

As he ambled over to us, I put him at about six foot eight and 350 pounds. He just seemed to take up space, swallowing up the air around him. A black baseball cap sat on his boulder-size head, an unruly Fu Manchu beard encircled his mouth. A green tank top exposed long, muscled arms and denim shorts hung to his knees. Dirty sandals attempted to corral feet, which looked more like small pontoon boats.

"Hey, Pete," he said in a gravelly voice. "Takin' a break?"

"Nope, we're done," Pete said, standing. "You know Deuce?"

Woody fixed me with a massive grin. "Can't say that I do." He extended a massive hand. "Woody Norvold."

I stood and we shook hands, his grip surprisingly dainty considering he looked like he could lift the earth. "Deuce Winters."

"Oh, sure, sure," he said, nodding. "Football player extraordinaire. Dead-body finder."

Everywhere I went, people gave me new suggestions for business card slogans.

"Excuse me a sec, will you, boys?" he said, sliding past us. "I'm starving and I need a quick snack. Be right back." He strode over to the stand.

"Told you you couldn't miss him," Pete whispered. "He's like an eclipse."

"How have I never seen that guy in Rose Petal?"

"He lives over in Brecker."

"Still."

Woody lumbered back out, a bratwurst in each hand. No buns. Just brats, held like hammers.

"So. Lotta excitement out here today, I guess," he said in between bites.

Pete and I both nodded.

"Good to see they didn't shut us down," he said, polishing off one brat and starting on the other. "No food would be a tragedy."

I wasn't sure if he meant no food for the fair or for himself. The 4-H stand was the only one that served anything substantial, but there was still the popcorn place, the cotton candy cart, the ice cream "shoppe," and the corn dog vendor. You could get anything battered and fried there: Oreos, Snickers, whole pickles, bacon, probably even bubble gum.

"Board still meeting tomorrow night, Woody?" Pete asked.

"Oh, yeah. Sure. It's a tradition."

"Like Bruce's wig," I said.

They both looked at me, confused.

"Never mind," I said.

Woody finished the second sausage and wiped his greasy hands on his shorts. "Anyway, yeah. Meeting's tomorrow night at seven."

"What goes on at the meetings?" I asked.

"Board stuff."

"Which is?"

Woody rolled his massive shoulders. "Just board stuff. Votes. Discussions. That kinda stuff. People will make some complaints about the fair and want them fixed this year. They'll make suggestions for next year. Most of it'll be nonsense, but there might be a good nugget or two in there. And I'd imagine there'll probably be some talk about George tomorrow now, too."

"Did you know him?" I asked. "George?"

Woody rubbed his huge chin. "You could say that. He was around here a lot. Nice enough fellow. I liked him." He paused for a moment, considering something somewhere in his massive skull. "But we didn't hang out together or nothing. We didn't get together on Sundays to watch football or go hunting. So I knew him. But we weren't all buddy-buddy."

His answer was nearly as convoluted as Bruce's,

and both of their hemming and hawing started to raise some more questions in my mind.

He glanced at the watch on his wrist. "I gotta get running, boys. Gotta check on the other stands and make sure everything's running smooth." He grinned. "And maybe grab something else to eat. Good to meet you, Deuce. See you later, Pete."

He took a couple of steps away from us, then stopped.

"You know, I really wasn't friends with George," he said, looking at me.

"Sure," I said. "I understand."

He blinked several times, something passing through his eyes, and he rubbed at the Fu Manchu again. "Yeah. More like I was *aware* of him."

8

"They both said *aware,*" I said. "Don't you think that's odd?"

Julianne and I were standing at the bottom of a massive slide, which Carly was about to go down for the ninety-seventh time. It was the safest looking ride at the fair and the only one she could get me to agree to letting her go on.

"They're *all* odd," she said.

"Yeah, okay. But I mean they used exactly the same word to describe how they knew him. Or how they *didn't* know him. Don't you think *that's* odd? Even more odd?"

Carly bounced down the slide, giggling the entire way. She hit the bottom, scrambled to her feet, and sprinted to the stairway to go up again. I watched it bounce a little as she bounded up, and tried not to envision the whole thing crumpling to the ground.

"The only thing I think is that if this kid

doesn't get out of me soon, I'm going to reach up there and pull it out myself," Julianne said, a hand on her enormous belly.

"I don't think that's physically possible."

"And I think you are treading on thin ice with a massively irritated pregnant woman." She frowned at me. "You promised me you wouldn't get involved."

I held out the lemonade I'd bought and she grabbed it from me, sucking hard on the straw.

"I'm not involved," I said. "I was just part of a conversation and I'm just making some . . . observations."

"Those observations usually get you in trouble." She handed the empty cup back to me and I tossed it in the trash.

"I just think it's weird."

Carly bounced down again and sprinted for the stairway.

"Last time!" I yelled.

She made a face at me and started up the steps.

"Well, it is weird," Julianne said. "But the whole thing is weird. You found a guy in a freezer. And I feel confident in saying they are all working with limited vocabularies. Maybe they just learned the meaning of *aware*."

"Ha. But what if they're ripping everyone off? Including 4-H?"

"I think my ankles are going to explode," she said, walking in place, her hands braced on her lower back. "Well, then, if they are embezzling, that's not good."

"I wanna go to the meeting," I said. "Just to listen to them. Pete thinks I'd enjoy it."

She shook her head. "No."

"Come on. One night. I promise not to say a word."

"You promised to stay out of it and it seems like you are practically in the middle of it already."

"I promised to stay out of George Spellman's death. This is totally unrelated."

She glared at me. "Do you even believe the words that come out of your mouth?"

Carly reached the bottom of the slide again.

"Okay, you're done!" I yelled.

"One more!" she yelled back.

"One more, that's *it*!" I told her.

"Which means, like nine more," Julianne said.

"I just wanna hear what goes on at these meetings," I said, ignoring her. "I'm not inserting myself into Spellman's death."

She glanced sideways at me, shaking her head. I knew I was driving her a little nuts, but I was genuinely curious. The fair was a big deal in Rose Petal and if people were screwing around with it, I wanted to know. It wasn't just that anyone associated with the fair might be losing money. The fair had been around for as long as anyone could remember and there were tons of Rose Petal residents who poured their hearts into the week to continue the tradition.

If someone was undermining that, people needed to know.

"You'll find a way to go even if I say no," Julianne sighed. "So just go."

"I won't say a word," I said. "I promise."

"Yeah, yeah, yeah. Whatever," she said, rolling her eyes. "Just don't expect me to bail you out if you get arrested or something."

"I'll take cash with me."

Carly was at the top of the slide and I walked to the bottom. She frowned at me, then jettisoned herself down the slide. She tried to scoot by me, but I grabbed her and picked her up. "Nope. Said that was the last time."

"But, Daddy!"

"No buts. It's time to go."

Her bottom lip quivered and tears formed in her eyes. "I wanna keep sliding!"

"Maybe tomorrow."

She let loose with a bloodcurdling howl and burst into tears. People in all directions turned to look and immediately gave me the raised eyebrow, wondering what I had done to make this cute little girl scream her brains out.

I looked at Julianne. "We're really gonna have another one of these?"

"Yeah," she said, grinning evilly. "And I hope it has a penchant for making one certain stay at home dad's life a little more uncomfortable."

She *really* needed to get that kid out.

9

"I do not understand why anyone would pay me to dig holes in my backyard," my father said.

We'd been home an hour before my mother and father had barged in the front door, my mother because she'd gotten wind that Carly was upset over something at the fair and my father because someone was apparently offering him cash to mess up his yard. Julianne was flat on her back on the sofa, her feet in my lap, feigning sleep, probably relishing the fact that I was having to deal with them when I just wanted to pass out.

"What exactly are you talking about?" I said, reaching for the beer I'd set on the end table.

He frowned at me from his spot in the easy chair. "Have you not been listening?"

"Actually, no. I haven't." I took a long gulp from the bottle. "You tend to ramble on about nothing and I find that it's easier to tune out and pretend I've listened than to actually try to follow what you're saying. I started doing it back in high school, actually."

His frown turned to more of a snarl. "They want to dig in the backyard."

"Who?"

"The gas people."

"People made of gas? How can you see them?"

His face screwed up with irritation. "Pammy! Where are you?"

Julianne's fingers dug into my thigh, but her eyes remained shut. She should've been an actress instead of an attorney. I wasn't sure whether she wanted it quiet or she was enjoying the conversation and wanted me to know it.

My mother walked into the room, holding hands with a red-eyed Carly, who was munching on an ice cream sandwich.

"What?" she asked my father. "And don't yell. Julianne and the baby are sleeping."

"Explain to your son about the diggers," he hissed.

"Well, they're this family on television that has, I believe, nineteen kids . . . ," my mother began.

"Not those crazy yahoos!" my father barked. "Those are the Duggars! I said *diggers.*"

My mother parked herself on the floor and Carly gravitated toward my father. He scooped her up and set her in his lap. She was oblivious, studying the ice cream in her hands.

"Oh, yes," my mother said. "The diggers. Apparently, we own some valuable land."

"How valuable?" I asked.

She shrugged. "We don't know. They want to come to talk to us about it. Or, rather, they want to come talk to your father because I'm entirely uninterested in the subject."

"Again, I ask—who exactly are *they*?"

"What was the name of the company, Eldrick? I can't recall."

"Taitano Resources," my father spat. "Like they're trying to confuse me or something into thinking they work with computers with a fancy name. *Please.*"

I didn't recognize the name of the company. I took a long drink from the beer. "I'm totally lost here."

My father settled back in his chair and wrapped his arms around Carly. "Taitano Resources is an oil and gas outfit. They want to drill on our property."

My parents had owned the same house on the same several acres since before I'd been born. My father had long maintained that one reason I'd excelled in football as a kid was because we basically had a football field for a backyard, where he had spent hours throwing me passes. They were among the early residents of Rose Petal before suburbia had encroached and started throwing up fancy new neighborhoods with gates and streets named after jewels and ponds.

"I got that much, thanks. Drill for what?" I asked.

"Natural gas," he said, making a face. "Apparently, we're sitting on it."

I stroked the sides of Julianne's feet. "So tell them no."

He glanced at my mother. "But they're offering us a lot of money. To lease the land. Or however those leases work."

"I find it hard to believe you don't know how the leases work," I said to him.

"Well, I know how they used to work," he said. "But we didn't really deal with them at the bank. We just held the money people made *from* the leases. But that was awhile ago and maybe they've changed. And I'm not about to use that danged Internet to go looking for information. You know how I feel about the Internet. That thing is evil." Dad had tried, unsuccessfully, to join Facebook, and it put him off the entire World Wide Web for good. He was convinced he could live off the grid for the remainder of his life.

I wasn't exactly sure how the leases worked, either. Texas laws were weird. When you bought a home, you either retained the rights to your land or you signed them away. In the development that we lived in, we had to sign them over as a condition of purchase. I had no doubt that my parents had retained every right to their property, given that they had lived there for so long.

I knew that oil and gas companies would "lease" the land from you, meaning that they could come in and drill and dig and do whatever they needed to do in order to get to what they wanted. The homeowners were paid—handsomely, in some cases—for the use of their land. They didn't receive a share of what was taken, but they were paid a sum for the companies to come in and do their work.

Or something like that.

"How much?" I asked.

"A lot."

"Like, buy-a-football-team a lot or send-your-grandkids-to-college a lot?"

He raised an eyebrow. "It's somewhere in between. And your wife has a good job, so your children will be able to attend college and you can continue to lay around the house eating bonbons and spending her money."

He never got tired of needling me about staying home and I never was able to stop it from irritating me.

"So do it, then," I said.

"But I don't trust them."

"So don't do it, then."

"You are absolutely no help."

"Probably not."

Carly finished the ice cream sandwich and jumped down out of her grandfather's lap, vanilla and chocolate smeared around her mouth. "Gramma, I think I need a napkin."

"I would say so," my mom said, smiling at her. She glanced at me. "They call it fracking."

"Fracking?" Somewhere, I'd heard the word. On a commercial, on the news. I'd always tuned it out because I didn't think it was going to affect me.

My father snapped his fingers. "That's right. Fracking. I couldn't remember the word."

"How they drill," my mother said. "Something with water and I don't know what else. And it's not supposed to be safe."

"It isn't," Julianne said without opening her eyes.

"Mommy's awake!" Carly said.

"She was never asleep," I mumbled.

"It isn't safe," Julianne said, opening one eye. "Pollutes the water table. Don't do it, Eldrick. I don't care how much they offer you. Won't be worth it."

"At least *she* knows something," my dad said, frowning at me.

"She knows everything," I said. I leaned down and kissed her stomach. "That's why I love her."

"Yeah, but there's no explanation for why she tolerates you," my dad said.

Julianne looked up at me, both eyes open, a huge smile on her face. "There really isn't."

10

After my parents left, I threw some chicken on the grill, tossed a salad into a bowl, and chopped up half a watermelon. The girls seemed reasonably pleased with my meal choice, devouring everything I put on the table and topping it off with ice cream from the freezer.

There was a certain satisfaction that came with having learned how to cook meals for my family. I'd always been able to grill, but I'd never had an appreciation for how hard it is to put together a complete meal every night until I actually had to do it when I started staying home. My initial efforts were poor, especially when I was sleep deprived during Carly's infancy. But I'd slowly improved and now I was at the point where I could open the fridge and put together something that would make both Julianne and Carly happy.

I liked that.

Julianne went upstairs to take a shower and Carly and I went outside to throw the football. She'd started to show an interest in throwing and catching things and I didn't want to do anything to stunt that. So I'd bought her a little Cowboys football, much to my dad's delight. Throwing it out in the front yard after dinner was becoming a nightly routine, heat indexes be damned.

"It's still hot," Carly said, stepping with her left foot and throwing the ball at me with her right hand, just like I'd shown her.

I caught it. "News said it was going to be hot all week."

"I get sweat on my bottom," she said. "It feels icky."

I threw the ball back to her and laughed. "Yeah, it does."

She caught it with both hands and fired it back to me. "Is it the same sweat I get on my head?"

"Yep."

"That's really gross, Daddy. I don't want to sweat anymore."

"We'd probably need to move from Texas, then," I explained, tossing the ball back. "Because living in Texas involves a lot of sweat."

She lunged for the ball, but it got away from her and fell in the grass. She picked it up and thought for a moment, her small facial features scrunching up. "Grandma and Grandpa would miss me if I moved."

The fact that she did not mention that they might miss *me* demonstrated that she perfectly understood the dynamic with her grandparents. "Yes, they would."

She shrugged and tossed the ball back. "Guess I'll just have to live with sweat on my bottom."

I was still laughing when I saw the Miata motoring down our street. I threw the ball back to her. "Here comes trouble."

She turned just as the car pulled up to the curb. "It's Mr. Doolittle!" She tucked the ball under her arm like a running back and sprinted to the curb.

Victor Anthony Doolittle hopped out of his convertible, wearing shorts and a Hawaiian print button-down shirt. Tiny flip-flops cradled his tiny feet and a straw Panama Jack hat sat on his bald dome.

He swept the hat off his head and bowed in a grand gesture. "Good evening, Miss Carly."

"Hi, Mr. Doolittle!" she said, giggling. "I like your shirt."

He straightened, and he was just barely taller than she was. He glanced down at his shirt. "It's one of a kind."

"A one-of-a-kind what?" I asked as I sat down on the front steps. "Wrapping paper for a pineapple?"

He ignored me. "How are you and your beautiful mother tonight?"

"I'm sweaty," Carly said. "She's upstairs taking a shower because she was sweaty, too."

He reached into his pocket and produced a tiny plastic animal. "I thought you might like this."

Her mouth dropped open and the football fell to the ground as she held out her hands. "It's a kitty!"

He placed it in her hands. "I saw all of those animals in your playroom last time I was here . . ."

"Littlest Pet Shop," Carly said, entranced by the plastic cat in her hands.

". . . and I thought you might like another one."

"I'm gonna go put it with the others right now!" she said, turning on her heels and sprinting for the house. "Thank you!"

She whizzed past me up the front steps and I heard the screen door slam shut behind me.

"How are you so nice to her and so rude to me?" I asked, holding up my hands.

"She's small and cute," Victor Anthony Doolittle said, walking across my lawn. "You're big and ugly. Duh."

"I thought it was because she's the only one around here you can actually look in the eyes without climbing a ladder."

He sat down next to me on the steps. "Your jokes are so tired at this point. At least try to be creative."

Victor and I liked each other. I think. We'd spent too much time together to not like one another. He'd roped me in as a reluctant partner in his investigating business and the reluctance had mostly disappeared. I worked part-time for him and it kept me busy during the downtime I had watching Carly. But our like for one another was almost always displayed in trying to embarrass and irritate each other.

"I'll try to be a *little* more creative," I said.

"Not subtle and not funny," Victor said, adjusting his hat. "So instead of working on your crappy stand-up routine, maybe you could explain to me why some battle-ax named Mama Biggs was calling me this afternoon looking for an update on her case."

"An *update*?"

"That's what she said you promised her."

I sighed. "I didn't promise her anything, Victor. She's somewhat insane."

"Yeah, the *crazy* sorta spilled through the phone."

I told him about George Spellman, the Biggs family, and the general nut-jobbiness that had surrounded the opening day of the fair.

"So I didn't tell her anything or promise her anything," I said. "She just assumed we'd investigate."

"Why does she care, anyway?" Victor asked, scratching at a mosquito bite that had just blossomed on his knee.

"I guess because of how it might affect the fair." I answered. "I'm not really sure. Like I said, she just showed up and assumed we'd investigate."

"Has to be another reason."

"I offer up the insane thing again."

He shook his head. "Nah. Something else. Why would she care? If it was just about the fair, she'd let the police handle it and issue a statement. Distance the fair from it. You know?"

That made sense. Susan Blamunski's rumor-spreading came to mind.

"What?" Victor asked, looking at me. "You know something else?"

I shifted on the steps, my back tying up a bit. "I'm not sure what I know, but I heard another crazy story that might somehow matter."

"Nothing is ever too crazy for this asylum you call a town," Victor said. "Spill it."

I told him what Susan had told me about Matilda Biggs and Spellman.

A smirk emerged on Victor's face. "Now we're getting somewhere."

I smashed a mosquito lurking by my ankle, ready to strike. "Hey, I'm telling you, this Susan woman might be just as nuts as the rest of them. She could've made it up on the spot, for all I know," I said.

"Easy enough to find out," he said, pushing himself off the steps and adjusting his hat. "I'll talk to Mama Biggs and work out the financials. She wants to ante up, we can visit this little meeting tomorrow night and see what shakes out."

I glanced up at the window, then back at him. "I promised Julianne I'd stay out of this one."

"You mean like every other case we take?"

I paused. "Yes."

He grinned as his little legs took him to his car. "So figure out a way to start apologizing to her."

11

"All of the food is rotten," Pete Boodle said with a frown.

The next morning, we were at the fairgrounds early. Carly wanted to walk through some of the exhibits before we had to work another food shift. But that now looked in doubt, as she and Julianne had headed to the open class building, and I'd stopped by the food stand to grab some coffee when Pete delivered the bad news.

"The new freezer they brought in didn't work," he said, hands on his hips, frustration all over his face. "Everything went bad overnight with the heat."

Several people were unloading the now foul-smelling freezer, stuffing garbage bags with hot dogs, pies, and hamburgers.

"What happens now?" I asked.

He shrugged. "Got me. Waiting on someone from the fair board to get here."

On cue, a caravan of golf carts buzzed up the dirt trail, headed in our direction, with Mama Biggs leading the charge.

She slid to a halt and was out of the cart before it stopped sliding. "What the heck is going on here?"

Pete repeated to her what he'd just explained to me.

She whipped her head around to Bruce. "Bruce! You plug that freezer in when you set it up here yesterday?"

Bruce and Matilda were now standing just behind Mama. Bruce was once again wearing his red wig.

"Yeah, Mama," he said, nodding. "I made sure it was plugged in."

"Well, then *why* isn't it working?"

"I don't know, Mama."

"Well, then, get your rear end over there and start looking at the compressor and tell me why it ain't working!"

Bruce hustled over to the freezer.

Mama muttered something about incompetence, then shifted her attention to Woody Norvold and the woman standing next to the golf cart they'd pulled up in. "Woody! How soon before we can restock?"

Woody scratched his massive head as doubt spread across his face. "Gee, I'm not sure. I can make some calls. But shouldn't we make sure we've got a working freezer first?"

"You let me worry about the freezer," she said, waving a hand in the air, dismissing him.

"You just get on your phone and get food here. We aren't going the entire day without food!" She glanced at the woman next to Woody. "And, Wendy, maybe you ought to get to making some pies or something. Don't just stand around being useless like usual."

Wendy rolled her eyes and settled her plump frame back in the golf cart. I wondered why Woody would let Mama get away with talking to his wife like that.

Mama turned her attention to me. "And what do you have for me?"

"Excuse me?" The coffee had been a bad decision. The cup burned my hands and the lack of creamer solidified its tarlike consistency.

"I'm not just paying you to stand around and look pretty."

I attempted to take a sip. "I wasn't aware you were paying me at all."

"Hello? We spoke about this yesterday. You report to me and only me. You've had twenty-four hours. That's plenty of time to come up with something."

I knew she was an elderly woman, but her demeanor and behavior were just flat-out offensive. She treated everyone with the same condescending, belittling attitude and I didn't care for it. Everyone around her seemed to take what she was dishing out.

I wasn't going to be in that group.

"Here's what I know," I said, tossing the coffee in the trash. "You spoke to me yesterday but never *asked* me anything. You just assumed

I'd do something because you wanted me to. That was your first mistake."

The small crowd of people around us began murmuring and several stepped away from us. Even Pete seemed to create some distance from me.

"Your second mistake was calling my partner before I had a chance to talk to him," I continued. "I'm going to make sure we charge you double at this point, *if* we decide to help you. And that's a massive *if* at this point."

Mama's eyes narrowed and I was pretty sure I heard Bruce whisper, "Dude."

"And your third mistake was just being rude. I don't like rude people. And you, lady, are unbelievably rude. If you think I'm gonna work for someone who treats everyone around her like servants, you are sorely mistaken." I smiled at her. "That's what I have for you. Ma'am."

Mama shuffled her feet in the dirt and fixed me with a steely gaze. The people around us were whispering, shaking their heads in disbelief at what they had just seen and heard. Apparently, no one was supposed to talk back to Mama Biggs.

Oops.

Mama set her hands on her hips. "You know what happened to the last fella who spoke to me like that?"

I shrugged, not caring.

"Nothing," she said. "Because no one's ever spoke to me like that." She glanced around at the crowd. "About time someone showed up with some guts."

No one seemed to know what to make of her proclamation. I was pretty sure they'd been waiting for us to grab each other and wrestle until someone gave up.

"Your partner did call me and leave a message," she said. "I haven't called him back. I will do so in the next half an hour." She hitched up her pants. "Perhaps after we've made those arrangements, we could discuss what you've learned."

The eyes in the crowd widened, shocked at what they were seeing. Mama's civility had stunned them all.

She walked toward her cart and slid in behind the wheel. "And you ever mouth off to me like that again, I'll shove my walkie-talkie in that big mouth of yours."

She winked and drove off in a cloud of dust.

12

"Word around the fair is that you and Mama Biggs had a little skirmish," Julianne said, her tongue lapping away at a massive vanilla ice cream cone.

We were sitting near the dairy building, the heat having returned once again, settling over us like one big sticky blanket. It was nearly lunch, but there was still no real food on the fairgrounds and ice cream was the best we could do to satisfy her hunger.

"I wouldn't call it a skirmish."

She eyed me over the quickly melting ice cream. "Fracas? Squabble? Scuffle?"

"Conversation."

"Not what I heard," she said. "I heard my husband told an old woman off."

I leaned in and licked the side of the cone, stemming a drip. "That old woman needed to be told off a long time ago."

"You big meanie."

"Where is our daughter, by the way?"

She studied the cone for a moment. "Who?"

"Our daughter."

"We have a daughter?"

"The pregnancy has finally eaten into your brain."

"If I wasn't so hungry, I'd smash this ice cream into your face," she said. "Relax. Your parents are here. They're spending ridiculous amounts of money on her at the games."

"My dad hates the fair."

"No, he doesn't. He pretends to hate the fair. But he truly loves his granddaughter. Some things trump other things."

That Julianne-ism about my father could not have been more true. He loved Carly more than just about anything else. It was going to be interesting to see how nuts he went over the new baby.

"So did you really yell at some old lady?"

I explained to her what occurred with Mama Biggs.

"I love how you promised to stay out of this," Julianne noted, arching an eyebrow over what was left of the cone.

"I'm not officially in it yet," I said weakly.

"Right," she said. She polished off the ice cream and began working on the waffle cone itself. "I'm sure Victor was over last night just to share recipes."

"Yes. For clam chowder. He loves clam chowder."

She rolled her eyes. "Whatever. You better

just make sure this in no way impacts the birth of your second child. Because if it does, you'll then be needing to ask Mama Biggs for a new place to live."

I reached for the hand that wasn't covered in ice cream. "Nothing will impact that."

"Oh, don't try to be all sweet and romantic with me," she said, wrinkling her nose. "You aren't carrying a small beast in your stomach."

"I know. You are. Thank you."

"Yeah, sure. Whatever," she said, finishing off the last bits of cone. She wadded up the napkin and tossed it at me.

I caught it in midair. "Can we talk about names?" I asked.

She stared at me, her eyes narrowed. "Yes. After the baby is born, I will tell you what his or her name is."

"That's not how it's supposed to work, Jules."

She raised an eyebrow at me. "Oh, really? So you're telling me that after forty-two weeks of nausea, heartburn, indigestion, and cramping—and not to mention stretch marks and saggy boobs that will never go away—I have to *share* naming the baby with you?"

Put that way, I wasn't sure I had any ground to stand on.

She nodded. "Yeah. That's what I thought. By the way, we're having sex tonight."

"That's quite the seduction."

"I don't have time for seduction," she said. "I need this kid out of my stomach. The kid that *I* will name. Pronto. Having sex with you is one way to make that happen."

I smirked. "Isn't that how we got here in the first place?"

"Shut up and come help me get up."

I helped her get herself turned around and into a standing position. She wobbled for a moment, her hands perched on her sides as she got her bearings.

"So, I know you're going to that meeting tonight, but you will be home in time to have relations with me this evening," she said. "That is an order."

"Yes, ma'am."

"Everything I've read says that's one way to pop an overdue kid out."

"So is induction," I reminded her.

She shook her head. "Seriously, Deuce. It's like you don't even know me. I am *not* being induced. I am having this baby naturally. Even if it kills me. Even if I have to have sex with you when I'm eleventy weeks pregnant."

"What if it doesn't work?"

She narrowed her eyes at me. "Then I'll blame you."

13

My father grinned at me in a way that I knew meant he was about to have fun at my expense. "Heard you've been making friends with Mama Biggs."

Julianne and my mom were walking Carly through one of the animal barns and he and I were sitting on a bench, watching the throngs of people stroll up and down the fairgrounds. A lot of them were complaining about the 4-H stand not having any food, while stuffing their faces with sugary confections and greasy fried concoctions.

"I'm not sure you'd call it friends," I said.

"No one's friends with that old codger," he said. "I'm surprised it wasn't her body you found in the freezer."

I ignored his sarcasm. "I think everyone's too afraid of her to do anything to her."

My dad nodded. "Probably so. She usually

has everyone on their heels. Glad you put her in her place."

"Not sure anyone can really put her in her place."

"Just not taking her crap in public was a good start," he said, still nodding. "I would've kicked your butt if you'd let her knock you around."

"Not sure you can get your leg up that high anymore."

"For your butt, I'd limber up."

I chuckled because I knew he probably would. "What's her deal anyway? She knows you."

"Oh, she knows everybody," my dad said. "And everybody knows her, in the same way that everyone knows the town bully. They know her enough to stay away from her."

"How do you know her?"

He yawned and crossed his legs. "Good Lord, I don't even remember how I met her. Had to have been at the bank, years ago."

"Yeah. She immediately identified you as having worked at the bank."

He shrugged. "That will always be my identity in Rose Petal."

That was true. He'd worked at the bank for most of his adult life, managing for almost thirty years before he retired. In a small town like Rose Petal, the bank was as much of a community hub as any other spot in town. He'd signed off on loans and mortgages for nearly everyone in Rose Petal. He'd opened accounts for nearly everyone born in Rose Petal. And anyone that needed a break financially? Well, he'd found a way to help them out, too. My dad didn't just live in Rose Petal. For a lot of people, he *was* Rose Petal.

"Can't recall what for, but I'm sure the first time I met her was there," he said. "Don't know why I would've had any other reason to associate with her." He waved a hand in the air. "Anyway, she was always in and out, whining and complaining about how we handled her money. Most of it was nonsense and it got so that the tellers would run for the back when they saw her coming because they were so sick of her antics."

"Who dealt with her then?"

"Most of the time, it ended up being me," he said. "Anybody that was a known problem, I'd usually handle them. I didn't like putting my people in those situations. And she was a chronic pain in the rear."

Before I could ask my next question, Susan Blamunski sauntered up to us, a smile nearly as big as her hair spread across her face.

"Well, well," she said. "If it isn't two of Rose Petal's finest gentlemen. How are we today?"

"We are just fine, Susan," my father said.

I nodded in agreement.

"Excellent," she said. "And have we learned any more about what happened with George?"

"No, we have not," I said, wondering why we were using *we* all of a sudden.

"I heard you and your little partner were investigating," she said. "Certainly you know something by now."

"I'm not at liberty to discuss, Susan."

"I heard you and Mama had a bit of a showdown earlier," she said.

"You have tremendous hearing," my father said, chuckling.

Her cheeks flushed. "Oh, you know what I mean."

"I don't know anything, Susan," I said. "There's nothing to report to anyone."

"Hmm," she said, clearly unsatisfied with my answers. "Well, 4-H is certainly taking a beating with all of this. I'm trying to get an answer now as to whether or not we'll have a working freezer anytime soon."

"You'd probably best get that answer near the food stand, then," my father said, still smiling.

"I suppose you're right," she said, a thin smile on her brightly colored lips. "Have a good day, gentlemen."

She strode off in the same direction from which she'd arrived.

"That woman is nothing but a mouthful of gossip dressed up in poor makeup," my father observed.

"Back to Mama Biggs," I said. "At the bank. What did she used to complain about?"

"Anything and everything," he said, frowning. "She always had cash deposits and she was always afraid we were going to miscount it or something."

"Lots of cash?"

He thought for a moment, then nodded. "Yeah, a fair amount. No pun intended."

I watched a couple with twins in a stroller walk by, looking at the map, wondering where to go first. I wondered if Mama Biggs's cash deposits were a coincidence or if maybe she really had been stealing from the fair for years.

"What do you know that you're not telling me?" my father asked.

"Nothing, really."

"Baloney."

"I'm hearing things about her. And about the rest of the board, for that matter. Just makes me wonder."

My dad folded his arms across his chest. "Son, people have been saying it for years."

"Saying what?"

"That Mama pockets more than her fair share of the fair revenue," he said with a wink. "That is not some new story."

"You think it's true?"

He sort of shrugged, and pursed his lips. "I don't know. Probably. Where there's smoke, there's fire, and all of that."

"Why hasn't anyone ever looked into it?"

"Like who?" he asked, chuckling. "The entire

board is made up of her family and her cronies. And, truth be told, the revenue generated by the fair isn't huge, so I'm not sure anyone ever had a reason to stick their nose into it."

I glanced around. The fair drew people from not only Rose Petal but the surrounding towns, as well. It was busy for the entire week. It was an institution, so I had a hard time believing it didn't bring in a good amount of money. I understood what my father was saying, but I didn't think it made it any less wrong. If Mama Biggs or anyone else in her family was taking money from the fair, it was time to stop it.

"What's the board selection process?" I asked.

My dad stretched his arms and stood. "Honestly, I don't know. She and her family have run it for so long, I don't think anyone's thought about that for a while." He made a face and raised an eyebrow at me. "And before you start poking around, know this. Running the fair isn't exactly an easy thing to do and no one's been clamoring for that job. Everyone has been pretty happy letting her run it. She may be a huge pain in the rear, but she's also done a pretty good job of pulling this thing off every year for as long as I can remember."

It was a good point. She may have been secretive and brash and not terribly likable, but her way seemed to have worked. Year after year, people kept coming back to the fair. People had fun. They enjoyed themselves. So while she wasn't going to win any popularity contests, she seemed to know how to organize and run a county fair.

But I was still curious.

"So before you blow up that meeting this evening, keep that in mind," my father said, cracking a smile. "You could end up driving a golf cart next year."

14

I grilled ribs for dinner and did the dishes in record time.

"Scoot," I said to Carly as I dried and put away the last of the plates.

She hovered at the table, licking her barbecue-stained fingers.

"Time for a bath."

She continued licking. "I'm giving myself a bath. Like a cat."

"I'm going to give you a bath," I told her. "Like a human."

She giggled and followed me up the stairs.

I started the water and dumped a capful of liquid soap into the tub as she stripped out of her clothes and dug around for her basket of bath toys.

"This guy is my favorite," she said, holding up a rubber duck wearing a cowboy hat.

Her favorite changed daily, it seemed. I

lathered her hair with special kids' shampoo. "Yeah? Why is that?"

"I don't know." She plunged it under the water and squeezed.

"Look up," I said. She did and I poured a cup of water over her hair, shielding her eyes with one of my hands.

I loved giving her baths. I loved taking care of her. There was nothing I'd rather do than be a dad and once again, I was grateful I had the opportunity to do that. To stay home and take care of my kids.

"Daddy?"

I rinsed her hair again. "What?"

"When will the baby be here?"

That night, if her mother had any say in the matter. But I didn't know for sure if it would work, so I told her, "Soon." It was the most accurate estimate I had right then.

"Are you happy about the baby?"

I set the cup down. "Of course I'm happy about it."

"Oh."

I looked at Carly. Her head was down, her eyes focused on the duck in her hands.

"Are you happy about it?" I asked. "About being a big sister soon?"

She shrugged her tiny shoulders. "I guess. I think so."

I repositioned myself in front of the tub, shifting my weight from one knee to the other. "Tell me."

She took a deep breath. "Well, it's just that

everyone's so excited. About the baby. That's all Mommy and you talk about. Grandma and Grandpa are always buying toys and clothes and stuff. For the baby."

My heart broke a little for my daughter. I knew it took a lot of courage to say these things, to talk about how she was feeling. And I also knew that she had absolutely nothing to worry about. I could have a dozen kids and still love all of them differently but the same. Every parent knew it.

But my daughter didn't.

I rinsed her off with a couple more cups full of water, grabbed the towel off the hook, and rubbed at her hair. On cue, Carly reached out and lifted the plug on the drain.

"I'm happy about it," I said. "Just as happy as I was the day you were born."

She looked at me. "Yeah? You were happy the day I was born?"

I smiled at her and lifted her dripping body from the tub. "Happiest day of my life. You were the best gift I ever got. You were the best baby in the entire world."

"I was?"

I toweled her off. "Yep. And you know what?"

"What?"

"You're gonna be the best big sister in the entire world, too. I just know it."

She nodded and smiled at me. "Okay, Daddy. I will be."

I hugged her and got her in her pajamas and handed her off to Julianne before heading out the door. And I made it to the fair board meeting with five minutes to spare.

The meeting was being held in one of the community rooms at the Rose Petal Library and I was surprised to see that most of the seats were already taken when I walked in. I'd gotten the impression that no one really cared about the board or their monthly meetings, so I wasn't expecting a crowd. But maybe George Spellman's death had stirred some interest.

I found a seat in the back row and Victor arrived a minute later, sliding into the seat next to me.

"Why the hell are there so many people here?" he asked, scowling. "Why aren't they over at the fair?"

"Got me. I thought it would be empty."

"I talked to the old lady," he said. "We're set with a retainer."

"That was quick."

He looked at me out of the corner of his eye. "Apparently, you made an impression on her this morning"

"I'm awesome."

"Whatever," he said. "And I already made some calls. There was definitely something going on with the daughter and the dead guy."

"Like?"

"Like I don't know yet," he said. "But my initial feeling is something was afoot."

"Afoot?"

"It's a detective word. You should use more of them. People might take you seriously then."

"I like it better when people think I'm your father," I said.

His scowl deepened, but he kept his mouth shut as the members of the fair board proceeded into the room. They sat at a long table at the front of the room and, except for Mama, they all looked a bit nervous. Mama sat at the far end, plunked down a stack of papers, and took stock of the crowded room.

"Well, seems like we're a little more popular than usual tonight," she said with a grin that seemed more menacing than mirthful. "We'll try not to keep you here all night."

A nervous chuckle drifted above the heads of the crowd.

She ran through some procedural things—approving minutes from the last meeting, simple committee reports, and attendance. It all seemed very by the book and there was nothing goofy or out of line in what they were doing. It looked just like any other meeting I'd ever been to.

"Now, we will hear from our treasurer," Mama said, and something close to irritation filtered into her expression.

Wendy Norvold shuffled some papers and cleared her throat. "As always, our financial report is fluid, due to the fact that the fair is currently in progress." She ran off a few numbers tied to surplus and expenditures. She glanced nervously at Mama. "We'll know more about what the town has earned at the conclusion of the fair, like always."

A hand in the audience went up near the front of the room. The board members looked at each other, unsure how to address this.

"You have a question?" Mama asked, clearly not happy with the interruption.

"Just curious about what the fair earned last year," a male voice said. "My daughter is doing a project for school on fairs and we had no idea how much money fairs make when they're open."

Mama kept her eyes on the questioner while the rest of the board members stared at their papers or their hands.

"We did just fine," Mama said. "Just fine."

"Oh, sure, of course," the man said. "But can you give us an idea of what the fair actually took in versus what it costs to put it on?"

"I just said we did fine," Mama said, raising an eyebrow. "Did you not hear me?"

"Uh, well, yeah," the man said, confused, maybe a little embarrassed. "We were just hoping to get some specific numbers, because I thought it was public information. My daughter . . ."

"Wendy!" Mama snapped. "You got the numbers?"

Wendy mumbled as she shuffled through her paperwork. "Uh, I'm not sure I have last year's financials with me this evening."

"How about your little girl just puts down that we took in a whole bunch?" Mama asked.

The crowd laughed nervously.

"Well, her teacher would really like specific numbers. . . ."

"Look, buddy," Mama said, pointing a finger at him. "Wendy just told you we don't have the numbers with us tonight. If you need your little numbers, perhaps you could leave a phone number and e-mail with her and she'll get back to you. That's all we can do and you'll just have to deal with that."

"Oh, uh, okay, sure," the guy said, sounding confused and a little sheepish.

"And do it *after* the meeting," Mama said, shaking her head. "We don't need to waste any more time tonight, because I've got a fair to run."

"What happens if the fair loses money this year?" another voice asked.

A loud murmur went up from the crowd.

Mama set her hands flat on the table. "And why in tarnation would that exactly happen?"

A man who I didn't recognize stood. He was a little older than me, with thinning hair and a growing belly. He folded his arms across his chest. "The food stand has already taken a hit and people in the surrounding towns are already whispering that this year is a failure. If they don't come to the fair, Rose Petal loses the revenue. If this is a nonprofit show, what happens if the fair week finishes in the red?"

Heads turned from the man to Mama, who did not look pleased in any way.

"We will be just fine," she said with a tight jaw.

"That doesn't really answer my question." The man frowned. "But I got a few other questions."

Mama smiled as if she were about to eat the canary. "Well, be my guest. Sir."

"The demolition derby was canceled this year," he said. "It's always one of the biggest draws. Why?"

"Liability," Mama answered. "Cost was too high. And we replaced that event."

"Yeah," the man said, still frowning. "With a clown obstacle course. That no one cares about."

"Clowns are funny," Mama said, glancing at her fellow board members.

They all nodded in agreement.

"But no one that I know has bought tickets," the man said, looking around. "I can't think of a single person I've talked to who is planning on going."

Most people nodded, including me. It had seemed weird to me when I'd read about it. I wasn't a huge demo-derby fan, either, but that put me in the minority in Rose Petal. It was one of the big draws of the fair each year. When it wasn't on the schedule, I'd expected there to be some blowback—and a worthwhile replacement. Clowns climbing walls and jumping over water and racing one another in their big clown shoes seemed . . . an odd replacement.

"That was lost revenue even before George's death," the man said, gathering steam. "Makes no sense."

"Thanks for your opinion," Mama said, her

mouth an ugly smile now. "We'll take that into account when we begin planning next year's fair."

"And that band you hired? Rusty Cow?" He shook his head. "My ears still hurt. I'm not sure that guy had ever sung a single day in his life."

Mama's mouth twitched. "They came highly recommended."

"From who?" he asked. "Deaf people?"

A few more nervous laughs floated through the air.

Mama just stared at the man.

"And the Ferris wheel hasn't been open at all" he said.

"Mechanical issues," Mama said, drumming her fingers on the table. "That is beyond our control and we won't risk the lives of the people in this town."

"Isn't that the most popular ride every year?"

She sneered at him. "I don't know. Why don't you poll the people in town and get back to me?"

"I don't need to," he said, unfazed by her tone. "I already know. You also denied the elementary school permission to do the snow cone booth this year. Why was that?"

"We are trying to create a healthier environment this year at the Carriveau County Fair," Mama Biggs said.

"Does she believe what she's saying?" Victor whispered in my ear. "Because, I don't."

I wasn't sure if she did or not, but I was with Victor. This guy was pointing out a lot of things that weren't adding up.

"Right," the guy said. "Because mini-donuts and fried everything are so healthy. People come to the fair to eat fair food."

The crowd again murmured, both in agreement and excitement.

Mama Biggs, however, was definitely not excited.

"Sir, I don't know who you are and I don't really care," she said, staring at him with eyes like lasers. "Until you have run the fair for two decades and actually have the experience to know what you're talking about, I'd suggest you shut your yap."

The man's face went crimson, but he didn't back down. "Well, maybe it's time for some new blood on the fair board."

Mama's face turned to stone. "Elections are at the end of every fair. You are welcome to submit your name for consideration."

"Maybe I will," he said, nodding. "Maybe I will. Because nothing you people are doing this year is making any sense to any of us."

The murmuring grew to actual conversations and people were clearly surprised and excited and confused at what had just transpired.

Mama smacked her hand down on the table and stood. "And now that we've covered everything, I move that we end this evening's meeting."

Matilda and Bruce both offered a meek "seconded" and the board hurried away from their table and out of the room, Mama still glaring at the man who dared question her.

15

The questioner of Mama Biggs stuck out his hand. "Butch Dieter. You're Deuce Winters, correct?"

We were standing outside the library, the crowd having moved out after the meeting but not in any hurry to disperse. Victor had disappeared to go talk to Matilda and I had sought out the questioner in the crowd.

"I am," I said, shaking his hand.

"Then I should thank you."

"Why's that?"

"Because you were my inspiration," he said.

"Inspiration?"

He nodded. "I heard about you standing up to her earlier today. Heard you didn't take any of her guff, that you stood your ground with her and called her out for being so obnoxious. Soon as I heard about that, I decided I was gonna stand up, too. So, thanks."

"Uh, you're welcome," I said, unsure of how to respond. "That was kind of a show in there."

He shrugged. "I guess. I'm just tired of that old bag lying to everyone."

"Lying?"

He nodded. "Yeah. Pinocchio has nothing on her."

"How do you know?"

He looked me up and down. "I heard you're working for her."

"Sort of," I said, unsure of how to put it. "My partner and I are looking into Mr. Spellman's death."

"That right?"

"Yeah. You knew him?"

His face clouded over. "George was a good friend."

"Was he? You weren't just aware of him?"

Butch nodded slowly. "Yeah. We were buddies. I was pretty shocked. We all were. He was a great, great guy. Deserved better."

"How'd you know him?"

Butch scratched his head. "Gosh, I've known him for a long time. We used to be neighbors until he moved awhile back. And he was in the club."

"The club?"

"Motorcycles," Butch said. "Actually, the guys are about ready to take some action. When something happens to a brother, it's serious business."

"A motorcycle club?" I asked, still unsure of what he was talking about.

Butch glanced around us and stepped a bit closer. "Look, I can't really talk about the club with someone who's not a member, all right? But trust me. We are looking into this and we will respond."

"Respond? How?"

"We're supposed to ride during the parade at the fair," he said. "We'll probably make a statement then."

"What kind of statement?"

"I can't discuss it," he said apologetically. "Club rules. But you can bank on it. The boys will respond."

I felt like I'd been dropped into some sort of weird B-movie version of *Fight Club*, but I let it go for the moment. "Were you serious about trying to get on the fair board?"

"I don't really know," he said. "I'm pretty busy at my office and I got some other stuff going on, but I really think she's ripping everyone and everything off."

"Why do you think that?"

"I'm an accountant," he said. "When I'm not out riding my hog, I crunch numbers all day. Nothing she says or does makes sense. I love this fair. Been coming since I was a kid. And I think she's got something cooking and it's not good for any of us. But I can just eyeball the amount of cash that goes through here and this fair should be growing. Instead, it feels like it's shrinking."

The crowd was finally starting to disperse. I agreed with Butch. The fair did seem to be shrinking and there really wasn't a good answer for it.

"So, maybe not me, but I think someone else needs to get on that board and break up her little family-run monopoly," he said, frowning. "It's not fair. No pun intended."

I thought for a moment. "George worked for the fair, right?"

He nodded. "Yes, sir. Every year. He was in charge of the grounds. Big job. And he did it for nearly free because he loved the fair. It cut into his other jobs, but he didn't care."

"What other jobs?" I asked.

"He had a landscaping business and did some handyman work," Butch said. "He was just one of those guys who could do a bit of everything. But come fair time, he'd clear his schedule. He liked being around the fair and being a part of the setup and upkeep. I mean—he loved it. He planned his entire life around it."

"He work a lot with Mama?"

He smirked. "What do you think? Of course. She calls the shots, so she was the one giving him his workload."

"He get along with her?"

"Actually, better than most," Butch admitted. "He just kind of laughed about her. I think he just liked working here so much, that he was willing to overlook all of her crap. He found a way to coexist with her."

Cars were now streaming out of the parking lot.

"Was George in a relationship?" I asked. "Was he married? Girlfriend?"

Butch's face went crimson just like it had during the meeting. "Hey, man. I can't talk about that kinda stuff."

"Why not?"

"It's against club rules to talk about other guys' girls," he said with a straight face. "That kind of thing could lead to bad news for me." He shook his head, as if he was reminding himself. "No, sir. I can't talk about that. My bros might find out and I'd have to answer to the rest of the PDs."

"The PDs?"

"The Petal Dawgs," Butch said. "That's the name of the club."

16

"So you think she's lying?" I asked.

Victor nodded. "Yep."

We were leaning against my minivan in the parking lot of the library. Most everyone had left and there were only a few cars remaining. Butch had excused himself, driving off in a late model Ford pickup rather than on a motorcycle like I'd expected, and I was left to ponder the validity of the Petal Dawgs when Victor came shuffling out of the library and motioned me to the parking lot.

"I didn't ask Matilda anything point-blank," Victor said. "I didn't want to freak her out. So I asked a couple of questions about how long she'd been on the board, that kind of thing. Then I asked how well she knew Spellman and she got real quiet."

"So you think Matilda was having an affair with Spellman, then?"

He adjusted the hat on his head. "I don't

know if it was an affair, or what it was, but there was something going on. I started asking her questions and she turned red like a tomato and that bozo in the wig came over to intervene."

"Bruce. The bozo's name is Bruce."

He waved a tiny hand in the warm evening air as if shooing away a pesky mosquito. "Yeah, sure, Bruce. Whatever. The dope in the wig. But he came over and tried to get all tough-guy with me and I told him if he didn't back off, I'd beat the crap out of him like I do everyone else."

"I'd like to see that list."

"Shut up. Anyway, she didn't give me a single straight answer about Spellman, and I felt like the rest of that group was eavesdropping the entire time. The old bag was definitely trying to listen in. We need to get Matilda alone and talk to her." He paused. "Actually, I'd rather you get her alone. I'm afraid she might sit on me and kill me. Jesus, is she big."

Before I could come up with a way to get her alone, the doors to the library opened and Mama emerged, leading her crew. The Norvolds walked quickly to their old pickup, Bruce and Matilda walked slowly toward an old SUV, and Mama was beelining right for us.

"What exactly am I paying you two to do?" she demanded, her eyes bearing down on me first, then Victor.

"Investigate," Victor said. "That's what you gave me the retainer for."

"Right. So what exactly do you think you're doing in there upsetting Matilda?"

"I wasn't upsetting her. I was asking her questions."

"That upset her," Mama said, her eyes bulging. "What exactly were you asking her?"

"That, ma'am, is exactly none of your business."

Mama's head looked like one of those cartoon characters whose heads were about to explode and steam started to shoot out their ears.

"Shorty, I am paying you and you work for me," she said through locked teeth. "Everything you do is my business."

Victor looked at me, bored. "Do all of you tall people just resort to short jokes when you got nothin' else?"

I shrugged. "Pretty much."

He turned his attention back to Mama. "We are investigating. When we have something to share, we will. Until then, who we question and what we ask them is our business. If you'd like to dictate every single question, then maybe you should be the private detective, instead."

I worried for a moment that she might try to tackle him and I wasn't sure how I'd intervene if that was the case. I definitely would've been on Victor's side, but I wasn't exactly sure how to appropriately remove an old woman from a midget. They don't teach you that in part-time private detective school.

"Maybe I'll do just that and ask for my retainer back," she said with a smug smile.

"I'll write you a check right now if you'd like," Victor said, fixing her with his own smug smile. It was fun watching them play chicken with each other.

Her smile dwindled.

She didn't know Victor well enough to understand two things about him: the worst thing you could do was threaten him, and he had more money than he knew what to do with. He wasn't kidding. He would absolutely have written her a check right there on the spot.

But, of course, she backed away from her threat.

"Well, when am I gonna know something?" she asked, waving a hand in the air. "No one seems to know anything. The police don't know anything and neither do you two."

"As soon as we know something, we'll let you know," Victor said, satisfied that he had once again swung an argument in his favor and gained the upper hand. "We still have more people to talk to."

"Who?"

"People who might know things."

She scowled at both of us and looked like she was about to say something, but instead stormed off to her car.

A brand spanking new BMW.

17

When I got home, Carly was already passed out after the long day at the fair. I checked in on her and gave her a good-night kiss on her forehead before heading to my own room. I remembered Julianne's orders from earlier and found her stretched out on our bed in cotton shorts and a tank top that barely covered her massive belly, reading a magazine.

As I undressed, I told Julianne about Mama's car and about the motorcycle club.

"I think I remember hearing something about the motorcycle club," she said while I brushed my teeth. "Bunch of guys going through their mid-life crisis together. Not sure I've ever seen them, though. But I think I remember hearing the tail end of some story where they got kicked out of Sturgis or something."

"That sounds about right," I said, lying down next to her. "This guy didn't exactly give off a biker vibe to me. He wasn't even riding a bike tonight."

"Was he wearing a leather jacket? With, like, a skull and crossbones on the back?"

"He's an accountant."

"So there were dollar signs and a ten-key machine on the back of it? How terrifying."

I laid my hand on her stomach. "How's baby?"

"Still in me." She sighed. "Carly asked if it was going to come out her size since it was staying in there so long."

I laughed and so did she, placing her hand over mine.

"You feel okay?" I asked.

"Like Shamu, but, otherwise, yeah, I'm okay. Tell me more about the meeting."

When I finished sharing the details, she was staring at the ceiling, mulling it over. "So was this Butch guy suggesting that they were sabotaging the fair?"

"I'm not sure what he was suggesting, but I think it could certainly be interpreted that way."

"That makes no sense, though," she said, shaking her head. "Why in the world would the board do that?"

I agreed, and it was what I had kept working over in my head on my way home from the meeting. It didn't make sense. If they were skimming from the coffers of the fair, what exactly did they have to gain from sabotaging it? I didn't see any way that that would work in their favor.

"I don't know," I said. "But the things he was saying? He was sort of right. All of those things are happening this year. Not to mention what happened with the replacement freezer. And it's hard to look at any of them and not think that they make for a substandard fair."

"Maybe it's coincidence."

"Maybe."

She rolled her head in my direction. "But what? I can hear the doubt in your voice."

"You know I don't really believe in coincidence," I said. "Lunacy in this town, I absolutely believe in. But coincidence?" I shook my head. "Almost never."

"But let's say this," Julianne said, putting on her trial lawyer hat. "Let's say the Ferris wheel really is broken. That's not hard to imagine. Those carnival rides look sketchy to begin with and I'd imagine that depending on the problem, they could be difficult and time-consuming to repair."

"True."

"And I could absolutely see the insurer declining to cover a demolition derby or raising their coverage fee so exorbitantly that it was difficult to pay."

"Okay."

"The elementary school snow cone thing? Who knows? Maybe some teacher said the wrong thing to her and pissed the old lady off. That could be any number of things."

"Sure."

"And no one counted on you finding that

guy in the freezer," she continued. "Except for maybe me, because these days it seems like you get in trouble as soon as you leave the house."

"Ha."

"But no one counted on that, so no one could've predicted it and what it's done to the food stand and overall attendance. And who's to say that new freezer was even working to begin with? Maybe it was an old one that sat around for years and no one ever used." She nodded to herself, liking her own argument. "So when you separate all of those things out, I think you could very much say that it's all bad luck and timing."

This is why she was such a good lawyer. She could divorce herself from the situation and look at it with fresh eyes, with no agenda or loyalty toward anyone else. She didn't just play devil's advocate. She brought the devil's advocate to life.

"So you think I'm being paranoid?" I asked. "You think it could all just be due to circumstance and that Spellman's murder could be totally unrelated?"

"Yes." She thought for a moment. "But, maybe not."

"What does that mean?"

"I think it means you should look at the fair and at Spellman's death separately," she said. "Focus on Spellman. If the stuff that's going on at the fair is related, I'd think it would reveal itself as you look at what happened to him." She paused. "Since you are now, very clearly, knee-deep in this case, after ignoring my pleas to stay out of it."

"Wait. I thought you gave me permission before to ignore your earlier pleas."

"Permission was never granted. You just ignored me. And I have learned to just live with you and your maddening ways."

I kissed her cheek. "Yes, you have. Thank you."

"Whatever," she said, barely suppressing a smile. "Now. You have a job to do. Or are you ignoring that, too?"

Of course, she remembered that. Pregnancy brain wouldn't get in the way of a mission. "You really are quite the seductress today," I said.

"Yeah, yeah, yeah," she said, rolling her eyes and pushing herself up. "Now roll over on your back so I can climb on top of you and try and get this enormous infant out of me."

18

The infant did not leave Julianne's body that night, but not for my lack of trying.

Twice.

She was up before me and already cooking breakfast by the time I made my way downstairs. The kitchen smelled like scrambled eggs and coffee.

"No luck?" I asked, kissing her cheek.

"None," she said grimly. "I'm moving to Operation Hot Sauce now."

"Is that my new nickname?"

She produced a bottle of orangish-red liquid from the fridge and held it up. "This is my new boyfriend."

"I'm a little jealous, but I think I can take him."

She unscrewed the cap and covered her eggs with the liquid. "I'm going to chase the baby out with hot sauce. It's going on everything I eat today."

"Everything?"

"Everything."

"I don't recommend ice cream, then."

She shoved a forkful of sauce-soaked eggs into her mouth. "Everything."

"You're sure that's okay for the baby?" I asked.

"The hot sauce?" She rolled her eyes. "Yes, Deuce. It's fine."

"Okay . . ."

She narrowed her eyes at me. "I know what I'm doing here. The sex, this . . . all are tried and true methods for natural induction."

"Sort of like the Drano test was supposed to predict we were having a boy when you were pregnant with Carly?"

The Drano test involved adding a few drops of the chemical cleaner to Julianne's own urine and, then, based on what color the urine changed to, we'd know what gender our child was going to be.

She ate another forkful of eggs. "That was an old wive's tale. I just thought it might be fun to try."

"You were halfway to ordering an entire blue wardrobe and engraving the crib with the name Carlos before the voice of reason stepped in."

"Yes, your mother did convince me I shouldn't put too much weight on that particular . . . test."

I sat down next to her. "I meant me."

"Hmm." She changed the subject. "Speaking of the crib, did you finally get it assembled?"

I cringed. The nursery had been a sore spot for the last month. Julianne had insisted we wait to work on the baby's room, mostly because she knew she'd want to keep busy with it during her nesting phase, but also because she'd been so busy setting up her new practice, she'd barely had time to think about it.

At the beginning of month eight, she'd tackled the guest room with a vengeance, hauling out the old furniture and stripping wallpaper in preparation for converting it into a nursery. She'd ordered a new crib and a whole slew of baby items.

Boxes arrived daily. Carly thought it was Christmas. I thought it was April Fool's Day.

"What on earth is this?" I'd asked, holding up a space age–looking trash can.

"A Diaper Wizard," Julianne had said.

"And it's magical how?" I'd asked as I examined the opening.

"It's supposed to keep diaper odors at bay."

"So do plastic Walmart bags."

"No, this is different," she'd said.

"Yeah," I'd told her. "This cost fifty dollars. Plastic Walmart bags are *free.*"

And then the crib had arrived. A crib that supposedly converted into a toddler bed and then a twin bed. I'd stared at the slats and springs and the 72-page instruction manual and thrown my hands up in frustration.

"Why can't we just use Carly's old crib?" I'd asked.

"Because Victor has it," Julianne had reminded me.

Yet another strike against the midget. His wife had recently given birth to their own baby, and in a burst of generosity—or insanity—we had given him the crib Carly had outgrown.

I'd studied page one of the instructions on the fancy new crib. "This thing is ridiculous. I could assemble a space shuttle quicker."

"The baby would probably love a space shuttle. You can do that after the crib. I'll call NASA now."

"The baby might be sleeping in a shoebox," I'd mumbled.

"What?"

"Nothing." I'd laid the instructions out in front of me. "This will probably take me a couple days."

A couple days turned into a couple months and it was still in a state of disarray upstairs. A shoebox was a distinct possibility. But I wasn't worried. I had big feet. The kid would have plenty of room.

Carly bounded down the stairs, already dressed in shorts and a tank top, and immediately made a face. "What are you eating, Mommy?"

"Eggs," Julianne said, her eyes watering. "With hot sauce."

Carly eyed her suspiciously. "Does it hurt?"

Julianne shook her head no, but couldn't produce any words.

Carly looked at me. "Is it to get the baby outside of her?"

"Yep."

"I don't think I ever want to have a baby," Carly said. "It seems . . . hard."

"Your mom is kinda insane right now," I whispered.

"What's insane?"

"Crazy."

"I'm right here," Julianne mumbled, her mouth full of eggs and burning fire. "I'm pregnant, not deaf."

"What are we doing at the fair today?" Carly asked.

"You and Mommy are working in the baby animal barn, I think," I said.

Julianne nodded. "Yeah. Would be a nice place to have a baby."

"Is the food stand open yet?" Carly asked.

"I'm not sure, kiddo," I said, standing up. "I'm gonna head over there now and find out what the deal is today."

"Can I come with?"

"No," I said, running a hand through her hair. "I need you to stay here and keep your mom company. In case she sets herself on fire."

"I know where the fire extinguisher is!" Carly exclaimed. "It's in the closet!"

"Excellent," I said. "If you see any flames around her body, you pull the pin on that thing and aim it at the middle of Mommy."

"Okay."

Julianne ignored us and continued plowing through the eggs, sweat streaming down her forehead, determined to pop that kid out.

19

I was halfway to the fairgrounds when I realized someone was following me. And they weren't doing a very good job of staying inconspicuous. Amateurs.

I'd showered and dressed and put gas in the minivan and was in the middle of town when I spotted a black Toyota Prius right behind me. I'd noticed it at the gas station because it was at the pump across from me and the college kid driving it hadn't seemed to know where to put the gas in. He'd puttered around it nervously, before finally sticking the nozzle where it belonged. When I'd finished at the pump, he'd hurriedly done the same, spilling gasoline on the ground and hustling to get in his car.

The car had stayed right behind me since I'd left the station and as I pulled into the fairground parking lot, it turned in, too, parking several rows over from me, despite the fact that there were only a few cars in the lot.

I took my time getting out and watched the Prius driver get out, along with a girl on the passenger side. Both looked to be college aged and both wore sunglasses. He had on plaid Bermuda shorts, a tank top with a peace symbol in the middle of it, and slip-on Vans. The girl wore her long blond hair in a tight braid, denim shorts, and a bright green T-shirt with a design on it that I couldn't make out.

They both seemed unsure of themselves and I just stood at the back of the minivan, waiting them out. They whispered back and forth, shooting furtive glances my way, probably waiting for me to move.

I sat down on the back bumper of the van and smiled at them.

They whispered some more and then finally headed my way.

"Was wondering if we were going to stand here all day and just look at one another," I said when they got close.

They exchanged glances again and the girl cleared her throat. "We know who you are."

At least they hadn't tried to deny that they were following me. "Okay."

"The private detective," she said. "Right?"

"You said you knew who I was. You tell me."

"You're Deuce Winters," the guy said.

"And who are you two?"

Nervous glances again.

"I'm Dorothy," the girl said. "He's Scarecrow."

"Really."

"As far as you know."

"The Tin Man couldn't make it? He have to work today, or is he in the back of the Prius with the flying monkeys?"

They both shuffled their feet. They may have followed me, but they were absolutely not professionals.

"Okay, Dorothy," I said. "I'll play along for now. Why were you following me?"

"We have information for you," Dorothy said.

"Yeah? Okay. Information would be great. I'm always looking for information. It's just like free money."

"Hey, man," Scarecrow said, trying to give me a hard stare. "She's serious. We're serious."

I gave him my own hard look. "You just named yourselves after characters from *The Wizard of Oz* and looked like you wanted to pee your pants when I sat here and waited you out. Excuse me if I don't take you too seriously right now."

"Talking to you could get us in trouble," he said, lowering his voice, despite the fact that we were the only ones in the parking lot.

"How's that?"

He looked at Dorothy.

"We have information about George Spellman," Dorothy said.

I hesitated. "Have you shared it with the police?"

They both made faces like I'd force-fed them lemons.

"Man, the pigs are a joke," Dorothy hissed. "They'd never believe us. They hate us."

I didn't think I'd easily believe someone who called the cops "pigs," either. They'd been watching too many bad seventies movies. "Why's that?" I asked.

Scarecrow puffed out his chest. "We're anti-establishment, man."

"What does that mean?"

"Never mind what it means," Dorothy said. "We don't have much time."

"Why not?"

"He's got a class at noon and I have to get to work," she said. "I'm a server at Chili's."

"Very anti-establishment," I observed.

"Do you know what fracking is?" Dorothy asked, undeterred by my observation.

It was the second time in a couple of days that the term had come up. It was apparently a very hot topic and something I really needed to learn more about.

"I know a little bit about it, but not a ton. Why?"

"Because Rose Petal is under attack, man," Scarecrow said.

Dorothy nodded in agreement. "Attack is

exactly the right word. They're looking to destroy the environment."

"Who exactly are *they*?"

"The frackers!" she said. "The gas companies that want to drill and contaminate our water supply and our air and our food."

"Everything, man," Scarecrow said, shaking his head sadly. "They want to destroy everything."

"There are currently six companies seeking to obtain drilling rights in Rose Petal right now," Dorothy said. "Six. Did you know that?"

"I did not."

She shook her head as if she knew I would never know that. "Six companies who want to come in here, bring their trucks in, drill massive holes in the ground, and start screwing everything up."

"Everything, man," Scarecrow said again, with the same sad headshake.

"Okay," I asked, completely confused. "But what does this have to do with George Spellman?"

They looked around, cautious and paranoid. Dorothy looked at Scarecrow and he finally gave a nod to her.

"He was a part of our group," she said, quietly.

"Your group?"

She nodded. "Yeah. George was in C.A.K.E. with us."

"Cake?"

"C-A-K-E," she said. "Citizens Against Killing the Environment."

20

Cars were beginning to stream into the parking lot, filling in the rows around us.

"We formed C.A.K.E. about a year ago," Dorothy explained. "We just got tired of all the abuse going on and decided to do something about it."

"What do you mean, abuse?"

She shrugged. "Climate change is real, okay? If we don't start taking steps to protect the environment, find other fuel resources, and recycle the products we use, the entire planet is endangered. And that isn't me just spouting off. That's a fact." She glanced at Scarecrow. "So think globally, act locally. We decided to get a group together that would take some action and make people aware."

Her speech was good. I couldn't tell if it was because it was well rehearsed or because she was well informed. I was leaning toward well informed. She seemed a bit sharper than her partner. And her alias was at least a real name.

"What exactly do you do?" I asked.

"We *protest,*" Scarecrow said. "Man, we protest."

"How? Where? Who?"

"Right now, we're kind of a . . . loose group," Dorothy said, adjusting her sunglasses on her nose. "Our membership is growing. We hold some information sessions about things people can do, but they aren't well attended, to be honest. So sometimes we get together and protest. Peaceful demonstrations."

"How many members do you have?"

She shuffled her feet. "About twenty. We're trying to grow it, but it's not easy. People either don't want to get involved or they don't believe."

I was expecting to hear that it was just her and Scarecrow, so I was actually surprised.

"We do petitions, hold rallies, things like that, too," Scarecrow said.

"And George was part of your group?" I asked, a little disbelieving.

They both nodded vigorously.

"George was awesome," Dorothy said, a wistful smile on her face. "He came to a meeting we had about three months ago and he knew a lot about a lot. He was really into recycling. He knew about composting. He was really well read. He just was into it and he didn't treat us like a bunch of crazy hippies. He was older than most of the rest of us, so he wasn't so much our leader, but he was kind of a . . ."

"Mentor," Scarecrow said.

"Yeah, mentor. That's a good word. He helped us find info and he would run meetings when I couldn't be there," Dorothy said. "Like when I had to be at work at Chili's or Luke . . ."

"Jesus, Emily," Scarecrow/Luke whispered under his breath.

Her face reddened. I wasn't sure if it was because she'd given his name away first or that I now knew hers, too.

"It's okay, Dorothy," I said, nodding and pretending I didn't catch her real name. "Go on."

Despite the stupid names, I sort of liked them.

"I mean, when Scarecrow had a frat meeting," she said. "Or something like that. The point is, George was involved and he helped us and he was really concerned about what was going on in Rose Petal. He took it seriously."

"How did he help?"

"He'd put information together," she explained. "Make it so we could understand it. He totally broke down fracking and the dangers it posed to people, especially in Rose Petal. When people got fired up, he'd calm them down. He believed in nonviolent protest all the way. He didn't want us to do anything stupid. But he really believed in the idea of making people aware."

First, the Petal Dawgs. Now, C.A.K.E. George

apparently had a lot of outside interests. I'm not sure why, but I hadn't pictured him being involved in community activities. I saw him just doing his job and that was it. I was probably guilty of thinking that about a lot of folks in Rose Petal. It was hard envisioning them as anything other than what I saw them as on a daily basis.

"And last week," Dorothy said, glancing at Scarecrow, "he said something bad was happening in Rose Petal."

"What was it?"

"He wouldn't tell us," she said, shaking her head.

"Yeah," Scarecrow said. "He said he wasn't ready to involve us yet."

"You ask why?"

"Yeah, of course," Scarecrow said, annoyed. "But he wouldn't say anything. Just said he'd learned something and he was upset and he needed to find out more before he told us."

"Have you talked to the police?" I asked.

They both made faces as if I'd spit on their shoes.

"No," Dorothy said. "Like we said, we don't talk to the pigs. And, let's face it. The police here in Rose Petal are kind of lame."

Hard to argue with that, especially after my conversation with Sheriff Cotter, but still.

"George was murdered," I said, looking at

both of them. "That's the kind of info they can use to help find out who killed him."

"Or they can ignore us and treat us like crap," Scarecrow said, scowling. "Bad enough that we're college kids. But add in the fact that we're doing what we're doing and it seems like everyone thinks we're stupid. That's why we came to talk to you."

"Me? Why?"

"We heard you were looking into his death," Dorothy said. "And people say nice things about you. We didn't know who else to go to." She paused. People said nice things about me? "You are investigating his death, aren't you?"

I hesitated, then nodded.

"So we thought you should know," Dorothy said. "I wish it was more. George deserves better than what happened to him. Maybe whatever he knew was the reason for him getting killed. I don't know. But the way he acted?" She glanced at Scarecrow. "It seemed like a super big deal."

Scarecrow nodded an affirmation.

I watched the cars line up in the grass-lined lot like ants. Families poured out of their cars, kids bouncing with excitement, parents smiling and holding their hands, telling them to settle down and watch out for cars.

"I'll have to tell the police," I said. "And they'll probably want to talk with you."

They once again exchanged anxious looks.

"Just to interview you," I assured them. "They'll want to know what he said, see if you can remember any more details. I can vouch for you, tell them you're legit."

"We just told you all we know," Scarecrow said. "We don't know anything else. Really."

"Sure," I said. "But they'll want to confirm. They'll want to put it down on paper and add it to the case file. Dorothy's right. It might have something to do with his death and, if it does, the police might be able to follow it up. I'll follow it up, too, but the police should always know anything that might help them with a murder investigation."

Scarecrow leaned in close to Dorothy and whispered in her ear. They both glanced at me, but I couldn't read anything from their looks.

Scarecrow put his hands on his hips. "You'd have to be able to contact us. And be able to tell them who we are, for them to bring us in."

"Well, yeah," I said. "So maybe I could get a phone number or something? And I'd need your real names. Nothing's going to happen to you. I promise. The worst that can happen is that they don't take you seriously. You've done your part. That's all you can do."

"But what if they think we had something to do with it?" Dorothy asked.

"They'd have no reason to think that," I assured her.

"But you don't have our numbers," Scarecrow said, fidgeting. "Or our names."

"I have your first names." I had to admit at that point that I'd heard them.

"But not our last names."

"True. But I think you'd be smart to give them to me."

"You'll have to catch us," he said.

I didn't understand. "What?"

"Run!" Scarecrow yelled and they both took off sprinting across the grass lot, looking back over their shoulders to see if I was chasing them.

I was not.

I was just standing there, wondering for the millionth time if they added crazy to the water in Rose Petal or if everyone here was just born that way.

21

Before I could get into the fairgrounds, I was intercepted by an unfriendly face.

Sheriff Cotter adjusted his sunglasses. "Son, I think that maybe you have a memory issue."

He'd seen me coming toward the main gate and went from sitting in his lawn chair—de facto security—to standing up and hitching up his belt.

"Why is that?" I asked.

"Remember that conversation we had?" he asked, tilting the brim of his cowboy hat up slightly. "About not investigating until the fair closed?"

"Vaguely," I said.

"Son, I'm not messing around here," he said. "I specifically asked you to leave it alone until the festivities were over with."

"Well, unfortunately, I was hired to check

into George's death," I said. "I'm being careful to not disturb the fair in any way."

"The point is that I asked you not to," he said.

"I know you did," I said. "And I'll be honest with you, Sheriff. That didn't really make much sense to me."

"That right?"

"Well, maybe not about me doing the investigating. The part that didn't make sense was you letting a criminal act go unlooked at for a few days," I said. "Can't imagine that's the best way to go about it."

He sucked on his teeth for a moment. "That because you've got all that police experience?"

"I've never been a police officer."

"Exactly," he said, smiling. "So you probably shouldn't be thinking you know what I should be doing."

I nodded. "Probably not. But I'm curious what state law enforcement would think of that practice. Like, say, if I called the Texas Rangers later on today and let them know that you're sitting on a possible homicide. I wonder what they'd say."

The smile vanished. "Are you threatening me, son?"

"I'm just making an observation," I said.

"I'd suggest not making those, then."

"Or?"

"Or you'll be sorry," he said, raising an eyebrow behind the sunglasses.

"So I should let Mama know you don't want me doing anything about George's death?" I said.

He shuffled his feet against the dirt and hay on the ground. "Mama? What does she have to do with any of this?"

"She's the one that hired me," I said. "And she's the one who told me that if anyone gave me any trouble, I should let her know. And this right here? Sorta seems like you're giving me trouble."

He sighed. "Mama hired you?"

"Yes, sir."

He tilted the brim on his hat back down. "Well, that makes it all a little different now. Wish she'd tell me things when she changes her mind."

"Changes her mind?"

His mouth twisted, but he didn't say anything.

"She the one who told you to hold off on investigating?"

His mouth twisted tighter. "We have a standing agreement."

"What exactly is that?"

"Anything bad happens at the fair, she asks me to wait until it's over," he said. "I work around it. But I don't make a lot of noise."

"Why?"

"So it doesn't screw up the entire week," he answered. "One bad week here and it can have a trickle-down effect on the entire town. So it's not like I've just been letting the thing sit. I've just been very quiet about it. If I'm stalking the fairgrounds, asking every single person questions, it's gonna look a whole lot less friendly than normal. People will stay away. They'll talk. It'll mess up the whole week."

I didn't disagree with him, but it was still hard to see how that took precedent over a murder investigation.

"I pulled prints from the freezer," he explained. "Body is being checked for DNA samples down in Dallas. Determined cause of death."

"Which was?"

He hesitated for a moment, then shrugged, as if saying it didn't matter if he told me or not. "Trauma to the head. Not sure what the weapon was, but looks like he took a blow to the back of the head." He shrugged again. "So I'm doing things. I'm just not doing anything that might ruffle Mama's feathers." He paused. "Probably why she hired you."

"How you figure?"

"You aren't wearing a uniform or a gun," he said. "You aren't as scary as I would be."

That made sense. Even if everyone seemed to know that I was investigating, it was still different than uniformed officers roaming the fairgrounds.

"And if she woulda just told me that she'd hired

you, we wouldn't be having this conversation," he said, frowning. "Sorry, Deuce."

"No worries, Sheriff," I said. "Sounds like we both got only part of the story."

He adjusted his hat. "Story of my life, Deuce. Story of my life."

22

Bruce—he of the horned, red wig—squinted at me from the back of a pickup truck. "You know who did it yet?"

I'd just entered the main gate of the fairgrounds and he was in the bed of the truck, a cigarette dangling from his lips and a very large squirt gun in his hands.

"Nope, not yet," I said. I pointed at the squirt gun. "And please don't shoot me."

He looked down at his hands and laughed. "Oh, no, man. This is for the parade. To keep everyone cool. I'm just getting some practice in. It's gonna be so danged hot. They'll be begging me to soak 'em."

I didn't ask what he was practicing on. "Ah."

The driver of the truck poked his big, square head out. "Yo, Bruce. Where we headed?"

"Hang on a sec, Willie," Bruce said, then to me, "So, no leads?"

"I'm working on a few things," I said, being vague on purpose. "Talking to a few people."

Bruce's expression soured. "Yeah? Like who?"

"Just people who knew George, that kind of thing."

"I don't think anyone knew him too well."

"Why do you say that?"

He shifted in his makeshift seat in the back of the truck. "I just think he was kind of a loner. Always seemed to be off by himself, never talked to anyone. Probably a waste of time to ask people about him."

"Actually, I've found a few people who knew him pretty well," I said. "So I think I can put some things together."

He leaned forward. "Like who?"

Bruce was awfully interested. "Just people he spent time with outside of his job."

"I don't think he did much outside of his job, man."

"Well, like I said, I'm finding some different things. We'll see."

"Maybe he got himself stuck in there," Bruce said.

"Stuck in where? In the freezer?"

"Sure."

"How? Why?" Buried to his neck in a pile of sausages?

The pickup idled loudly. "Maybe he was looking for some free food or something. Maybe the door accidentally shut behind him. Maybe he was trying to fix something. Who knows?"

"I don't think he would've crawled in if he was just looking for some food," I said.

Bruce thought about that, then shrugged. "I don't know. Maybe he was really hungry."

Bruce wasn't making sense, which wasn't really surprising considering that he was wearing a red wig with horns for no good reason. He didn't seem like the kind of guy you went to if you wanted, you know, common sense. He seemed more like the kind of guy you went to if you needed squirt guns and free beer.

"You seem to know a lot about George," I said. "But I know you said you guys weren't really friends. How's that?"

Bruce moved around like a mouse was running loose in his shorts. "I told you before, man. I was *aware* of him. That's all."

"Right, but you were just telling me how he didn't have any friends and . . ."

"Let's go, Willie!" Bruce hollered and cut me off.

The pickup lurched forward, kicking up a cloud of dust.

Bruce stared at me as they drove away, the squirt gun tapping against his thigh.

23

I was halfway to the food stand when I saw my father walking toward me from the other direction.

"What are you doing here so early?" I asked.

He frowned. "Your mother volunteered us to sit at some table. So now I have to sit there while she yaks at everyone that comes through."

"Fun."

"No, not fun," he said. "I'd rather be home, taking a nap. But I heard something interesting at breakfast with the boys this morning that I thought you might be interested in, too. I called your home but your wife, who is about to have a kid any second, said you had abandoned ship and were already here."

"You guys aren't boys," I said, ignoring the crack and digging in with my own. "You know that, right? You're old men who act like boys."

"Whatever," he said, rolling his eyes.

He had breakfast every morning with his

four oldest friends at the same restaurant and they sat there like the town elders and gossiped like their wives. While I made fun of them every chance I got, they did know what was going on in Rose Petal ninety-nine percent of the time.

"There's some rumbling that they're looking to move the fair next year," he said with a sly grin, because he knew I was going to be interested. "Did you know that?"

"Move it?"

He nodded. "You know that plot of land at the north end of the county, up near Denton? Was supposed to be some fancy schmancy development but then the money dried up and it never went through?"

"Vaguely."

"It's there," he said. "Trust me. The land is pretty usable. Needs some infrastructure and a few other things, but it's a good chunk of land."

"It could hold the fair?"

He shrugged. "Structures would have to be built because it's essentially vacant right now, but, sure. Plenty of acreage. I would guess that it's already zoned for plumbing and electricity, given that it was originally going to be housing."

I looked around. I'd been coming to the fair since I was born. I'd covered every inch of the fairgrounds. I knew exactly where everything was, including all of the secret hiding spots I'd discovered as a kid. I couldn't imagine it all going away.

"Who exactly wants to move it?" I asked.

He raised an eyebrow. "Who do you think? Your pal, Mama Biggs."

"Can she move it?"

"Here's the really interesting thing," my father said, glancing around. "Sure, she can move it. The fair board as the governing body can do whatever they'd like. And as you well know, they'll do whatever she tells them. But that land up north? It's for sale."

"I'm not following you."

"In order to move the fair, that land has to be offered up for use by whomever owns it," he explained. "Right now, it's still for sale. Has been for almost two years, since the developers went belly up. The developers still own the rights and they've been looking to sell it to recoup their losses. They aren't interested in leasing it, because they're starving for money and they need to get as much as they can as quickly as they can. But there haven't been any takers."

"So, then, how can the fair be moved there? Wouldn't the land have to be owned by the county or something to house it?"

He smiled. I'd seen that smile a lot over the course of my lifetime. It was the one that said, "I'm so far ahead of you, I can barely see you when I look back over my shoulder at you."

"Well, it would definitely have to be owned by someone, yes," he said.

I waited.

"Mama Biggs was at the bank last week," he said. "Applying for a loan. To buy that property."

I took all of that in for a minute, working it through my head, watching several families stroll by us.

"Ed told me this morning," my father said. "I wasn't even talking about your shenanigans."

"So she wants to buy the land so she can hold the fair there?" I said, trying to connect the dots. "Why?"

My dad shrugged. "No idea. But I thought it was interesting."

"Why would that appeal to her?" I asked, confused. "So the county would have to pay her to use the new fairgrounds? That makes no sense. She'd have to pay for all of the new construction, not to mention the infrastructure needed to turn it into a fairground. I can't believe that would be worth it."

"Well, since no one knows exactly what this rinky-dink carnival takes in each year, maybe there's more money in it than we know," he said.

"Who owns these fairgrounds?"

My dad paused. "The county, I'd assume."

"But you don't know for sure?"

He chuckled and slapped me on the shoulder. "I can't do *all* your work for you."

24

"You look perturbed," Julianne said.

We were sitting outside the 4-H building under an awning and Carly was off helping her grandmother.

"Perturbed?" I said, then shook my head. "No. Not perturbed."

She grabbed one of the hot wings from the paper boat in her lap and held it up. "Hmm. Okay. How about bewildered?"

"Are you just trying to use big words to confuse me?"

She gnawed on the wing. "Maybe. Whichever word you like, you are clearly preoccupied with something."

I nodded. "Yes. The impending birth of our child."

She dropped the empty bone into the boat. "Ha. Funny. But that is not what I see in your expression. And remember. Being, like, ten weeks overdue gives me incredible powers of clairvoyance."

"I don't remember hearing that at birthing classes for Carly."

She chewed on another wing. "That's because you're a man and your hearing is awful."

"I remember everything from birthing class."

She snorted. "Oh, really? So how did you promptly forget all of it the minute we walked into the delivery room?"

"I didn't," I said.

"I think your memory is just as bad as your hearing," she said. "It's the whole reason we signed up for the refresher class. Which was totally stupid and pointless."

The refresher class wasn't stupid and pointless. We'd dutifully gone for six weeks of learning and bonding with other parents-to-be. Six of them, actually. All of whom had delivered healthy, happy babies. The "reunion" had been last week. We were the only ones still incubating, much to Julianne's dismay.

I laughed and told her about my conversation with my dad.

Her nose wrinkled and she pointed another wing bone at me. "I think this town might explode if the fair was moved somewhere else."

"I agree."

"I don't see how they think they could make that happen," she continued. "It would still be in Carriveau County, but it wouldn't be in Rose Petal. Which would mean big losses for the local businesses. Gas stations, restaurants, grocery stores. They'd all take a huge hit."

It was a good point and one I hadn't thought of.

"They'd all pitch a fit," she said, grabbing the last wing in the boat. "Not to mention everyone around here having to drive up there. They'd all freak. People walk with their wagons and ride their bikes. And I can't believe it would be that easy to just up and move a county fair."

"But if it just takes a fair board vote and the vote is controlled . . ."

"That's what I'm saying," Julianne said, then licked a finger. "I can't believe it's just a single vote that would allow the move. I'd think there would have to be other approvals involved. Local government or something. Something in the original bylaws that would require multiple agency approvals to move something so vital to all of the local businesses."

I pondered how I might go about finding out that information while she cleaned the hot sauce from her fingers like a cat.

"And now I can't help but think this is somehow tied to George Spellman's death," I said to her.

She grabbed a napkin and wiped her hands. "Why?"

"Why? Because it seems like a really weird coincidence."

"Everything around Rose Petal is really weird."

"You know what I mean," I said. "It just seems odd that a dead guy shows up in a freezer at the same time the leader of the fair board is looking to maybe move the fair."

She thought for a moment, then squinted against the sun. "The key word there is *maybe*. You don't know for sure that she's looking to move the fair."

"My dad was pretty certain about her trying to buy the land."

"So? Maybe she's trying to buy it for another reason. Investment. Flip it. Who knows? It doesn't mean she's looking to yank the fair up. She's a sharp old broad. It might be for other reasons. If the developer is willing to dump it for a low price and she can get the money, maybe she just wants it to have it."

Even in the shade provided by the awning, the air was getting hotter by the moment and beads of sweat formed on my neck. "He said he heard rumblings, though. About her wanting to move the fair."

"There are always rumblings," she said, rolling her eyes. "This town subsists on rumblings. You know how many of them end up being false. I'm not saying it is or it isn't. But don't just make the assumption. Find out for sure."

I smiled at my wife. I loved everything about her. Her intelligence, her beauty, her rationale when it chose to appear. I couldn't imagine myself married to anyone else in the entire world.

"Just keep digging," she said, pushing herself off the bench, placing her hands behind her back to support herself when she was upright. "The truth will turn up. It always does, because no one knows how to bury it the right way in Rose Petal." Her eyes scanned the grounds, moving all the way from right to left. "Now. I know I saw the deep-fried jalapeños somewhere nearby. Walk with me and buy me a couple, husband."

25

I got Julianne her fried jalapeño—on a stick—and after we finished our short shift in the animal barn, we convinced Carly that it might be a good thing to go home for a nap, since she'd be spending the rest of the night at the fair with her mom playing games, while I went to poker night. She grudgingly acquiesced and Julianne scooted her on home while I stuck around to do some more digging.

I was making a mess for myself, grasping at too many threads and trying to weave them together. I needed to pick one and hang onto it until I got to the end. Since Mama Biggs was paying us to look into Spellman's death, I figured that was the thread that needed the most attention.

There was one person specifically I wanted to start with and I knew I'd find her on the grounds somewhere. I went to the fair board office to see if anyone knew where Matilda

Biggs was and got lucky when she was the only one in the air-conditioned trailer when I walked in.

Her automatic greeting smile dimmed when she recognized me. "Hello," she said.

"Hi, Matilda. How's the fair going?" I asked, weakly attempting small talk.

"We're hanging in there," she said, fiddling with a pencil on the desk top. "Things seem to be settling down at the moment, so that's good."

"Oh, good," I said. "Is this a good time? I'd like to ask you a few questions."

The pencil went flying out of her hand and smacked into the wall. "Oh, well, I've got a lot of work to catch up on here and then I need to get over to the barns. . . ."

"I know my partner talked to you last night," I said, not letting her finish. "I just want to follow up with some other things."

She glanced at the pencil on the floor, as if it might help her answer the questions, but said nothing.

"I'm going to be direct," I said, not knowing how else to get around it. "I heard a rumor that you and George Spellman were close. Is that true?"

She looked at nearly everything in the room but me. "Well, I was aware of him."

There was that word again. *Aware.* "I'm asking, were you more than aware of him? My partner seemed to think that maybe you were . . ."

"That little midget?" she said, her flabby cheeks flushing. "He was kind of rude."

"That's the way God made him, I'm afraid."

"He kinda creeps me out."

"You're not alone. But you still haven't answered my question."

Her cheeks flushed a little more. "Well . . . I . . . uh . . ."

"Were you having an affair with George?" I asked, throwing it out there.

She dropped her head into her hands, covering her eyes.

"Matilda, unless you killed him, I don't need to share this information with everyone," I said.

Her face shot out of her hands, her eyes wide, her mouth as open as it went. She tried to say something, but nothing escaped her mouth. She coughed and cleared her throat, laying her hands flat on the desk. "I could never have hurt George. Ever."

"Why's that?"

Her eyes glistened with tears. "Because I loved him."

26

Matilda unwedged herself from the desk, waddled around it, and opened the door I'd come in. She hung a sign on the outside that said OUT TO LUNCH, shut the door again, and turned the deadbolt above the handle.

She dropped onto the sofa beneath the window, the entire trailer shaking beneath her girth. "I don't want anyone barging in and hearing this."

I grabbed a metal folding chair and sat down.

"About six months ago, I was here late one night," she said, her eyes still watering. "I don't even remember what I was doing. Paperwork, probably. Anyway, he came by the trailer. He needed a key to one of the barns." She sighed heavily. "He was so handsome."

I could only picture George in his denim coveralls. Considering the last time I'd seen him he was blue and frosted over, I couldn't remember whether he was handsome or not.

"I walked him down to the barn," she said. "We aren't supposed to give out the keys to anyone, even him. So I took him down there. And there was just a . . . spark."

She was at least half a foot taller than George and a good two hundred pounds heavier. I was trying to imagine the spark.

"We were just talking," she said, her eyes elsewhere, lost in her memory of George. "We were in the barn and he grabbed me and kissed me."

Whoa. Awkward.

"And it was the most amazing kiss," she said, a smile creeping onto her lips. "It was electric. That man knew how to kiss. I have no idea where he learned, but he was incredible."

I was wishing I had called Victor and told him to continue questioning her. I didn't need these images in my head. But now I was trapped.

"And, before I knew it, we were on a hay bale," she said, her cheeks flushing again, but in a different way. "I was on my back, he was on top of me, and he pulled out his . . ."

"So you were having an affair," I blurted out loudly, before she could say anything else that would scar me for the remainder of my life. "You and George were a couple."

She giggled like a teenager and brushed the stringy black hair from her face. "After that night, we were. But we kept it a secret." Her face clouded over. "I figured Mama might not like it."

"Why not?"

"Two reasons," she explained. "One, she really doesn't like men. Does *not* trust them at all. And, two, she didn't want any fraternitying between fair employees."

"Fraternizing."

"Yeah. That. I knew it would make her mad. So we decided to keep it quiet."

"George was okay with that?"

"He said he was."

She was proving to me that there really was someone for everyone. I believed her when she said she didn't hurt George. She clearly seemed to me to be someone very much in love.

No matter how much it grossed me out.

"Okay, then. I need to ask you something else," I said.

She pushed the hair away from her sweaty face again and looked at me anxiously.

"I was told that maybe he was breaking up with you," I said. "Is that true?"

Her bottom lip quivered and her eyes filled. "Breaking up with me? Why?"

"No, no. Someone told me they saw you together and it looked like he was breaking up with you. You might've been crying or something like that?"

She thought hard for a moment, then shook her head. "He didn't break up with me. I can assure you of that. So I'm not sure what you mean."

I didn't want to mention Susan Blamunski's name because I was afraid it might cause more drama. But she was the one who'd told me about seeing Matilda and George together in the restaurant.

"Were you out together recently?" I asked. "Publicly? In a restaurant?"

Recognition clicked through her eyes. "Oh my God. Our anniversary."

"Anniversary?"

"Six months from that first night in the barn," she said. "I wanted to go out and celebrate. He was kind of surprised because of the whole keeping-it-quiet thing. But I really wanted to go out and I was really tired of not telling everyone about us. I wanted everyone to know we were in love."

I nodded. "So you went out to dinner?"

"Yes," she said, and something in her body language changed. She went from remembering a night out with a man she loved to being very uncomfortable.

"Something happened at dinner?" I asked.

"I really can't talk about it," she said, her voice dropping to nearly a whisper.

"Why not?"

"I just can't."

"But something happened that made you cry that night?" I asked. "I was told you were crying. That's why it may have looked like you were breaking up."

"Who saw us?" she asked. There was no malice in her question. She just seemed curious.

"I really can't say," I said. "But were you crying?" I gently pressed.

She nodded, but still didn't say anything.

"But you won't tell me why?"

She shook her head.

The air-conditioning hummed loudly in the silence. I waited her out. She was good at staying quiet and she just stared back at me, her eyes watery and sad.

"Matilda, do you want to find out who killed George?" I asked.

She looked at me, bewildered that it could even be a question. "Of course, I do. They took him from me. And I'll never get him back. I'll never love anyone like that ever again."

"Then you need to tell me everything you can about George," I said. "And that means you might want to tell me about that conversation, too. What upset you so much that you would cry on your anniversary?"

She closed her eyes and bit her bottom lip, thinking.

"I think you'd be upset with yourself if you had information that might help solve George's murder," I said. "I think you'd feel guilty forever. You might not think it's important, but it might help me figure out what happened to him."

She finally opened her eyes. "George had a secret."

27

Matilda pushed herself off the sofa, and peered through the blinds. "I can't believe I'm going to tell you this."

She let the blinds settle and returned to her seat. "I swore to him I wouldn't tell anyone. Because I knew he was in danger. That's why I was crying, you see. I didn't want him to do anything."

She wasn't making sense, but I didn't want to interrupt her.

"George was out here at the grounds one day, maybe a month or so ago," she said. "I don't remember the date. But it was early morning and he was coming to fix one of the sheds, I think he said. He liked to get up early and get here while it was quiet."

I nodded.

"There was a truck here," she said. "And he thought that was odd, because no one was ever here that early, not even Mama."

"Whose truck was it?"

"It belonged to some company," she said. "I don't remember the name. But no one was in it. So George took a walk around the grounds and found this guy out where the midway is."

She was killing me with her lack of ability to get to the point, but she had momentum and I didn't want to get in the way, so I just nodded again.

"He was from a gas company," she said. "And he told George that he was doing some marking or something. For when they could start digging."

"Digging? On the grounds?"

Matilda nodded. "Yep. He was from a company that was going to dig for gas. Though I don't know how you dig for gas. There was a funny word for it."

My mind flashed on the conversation I'd had with my dad and with my Wizard of Oz friends. "Fracking?"

She snapped her fingers. "Yeah, that's it. I made a joke about it, but George didn't think it was funny. Anyway, this guy said his company was going to dig on the fairgrounds. George, of course, didn't believe him."

"So what did he do?"

"Well, the guy told him they were going to start digging in May," Matilda said. "As soon as fair week ends. George told him he was crazy, that he didn't have no right to do that, that it was private property. And the guy just laughed at him and told him to get lost." She sat up straighter. "But anyone who knew George knew you couldn't just talk to him like that. So he told the guy to get off the property, but the jerk said no."

I waited.

"So George told him again to leave and the guy just walked off, still measuring or doing whatever he was doing," Matilda said, anger in her eyes. "George grabbed him and told him to leave. And the jerk punched him in the face." Her eyes watered again. "Knocked my George out."

I was trying to put it together in my head, but was having trouble fitting the pieces together. "So were you crying because he knocked George out? Because he hurt him? I'm still not clear on why you were upset that night."

She shook her head. "No. I mean, I did cry when he told me about getting punched. But not that night at the restaurant." She wrung her hands like a wet washcloth. "He woke up on the midway and the guy and his truck were gone. The guy left a business card on George's chest, like he was being funny or something. So George went to tell Mama about it. He called her, told her to come right over."

"Did she?"

"Yeah," she said, anxiety returning and her eyes flitting to the window. "And he told her. And she told him it was none of his business, to forget he ever saw the guy and keep his mouth shut."

I waited for her to continue.

"George was mad and confused," she said. "He didn't understand how she could tell him to forget it. It was like she didn't care."

I thought it was more than that, but didn't say anything.

"And then he figured that maybe Mama was going to let him dig on the fairgrounds, but he didn't see how that was possible," she said. "I mean, it's the fairgrounds, not somebody's yard or something. He didn't know why, but he didn't like that at all. So he decided to do something about it."

"What was he going to do?" I asked.

The tears came again. "I begged him not to. I knew how angry Mama would be and I knew he'd probably lose his job if he went against her. But George was stubborn." She smiled through the tears. "My George was stubborn."

"What was he going to do?" I asked again.

"He was going to tell everyone what happened with the gas guy and tell them that Mama knew," she said. "At the next fair board meeting."

"Which was when?"

She wiped at her eyes. "It would've been the one last night."

28

Matilda made me wait until the coast was clear before I could leave.

The early afternoon sun was in full effect, baking the entire fair and its inhabitants with more unseasonably warm weather. I shaded my eyes against the sun as it burned into my skull, which was trying to digest everything I'd just learned. Not an easy meal in any way.

My dad waved at me from a bench in the shade near the entertainment stage and I sat down next to him.

"I snuck away from your mother," he said. "And, you look confused."

"I think I am."

"Not the first time. Probably why I recognized it so fast."

"Ha."

"You should probably go home and check

on your wife," he said. "She might be having a baby."

I pulled my phone out of my pocket. No missed phone calls or texts. I'd been smart enough to turn the volume all the way up just in case.

I put it back in my pocket. "She would have called. She's fine."

"So what are you confused about now?"

"The fracking thing," I said. "At your house. Tell me about that again."

He looked at me, puzzled, then shrugged his shoulders. "They called me first. I told them to buzz off. Then a guy showed up at the door. Young guy, nice looking, all friendly and salesy. He knocked on the door and I was ready to push him off the porch. Until he told me the kind of money he was offering." His mouth twisted in thought. "I looked at the paperwork and it looked pretty legitimate. A whole load of cash to do a little digging on the north side of our property. We talked for a few minutes. Told me to call him when I'd finished thinking it over. I haven't done that yet."

People were walking by, water bottles in hand, waving at the air with fairground maps and programs, trying to cool themselves off.

"Remember the guy's name?" I asked.

He shifted on the bench and pulled out his wallet, thumbing through it. "He gave me his card. Told me he was the rep for all of Rose Petal. Made some crack about how he was going to be the fracking king of Rose Petal." He pulled out a card. "Here it is. Corey Stewart."

He handed me the card. It was a simple rectangle made of white cardstock. His name was on there, along with a simple logo for Taitano Resources, a phone number, and an e-mail.

"Mind if I keep this for a while?" I asked.

"Why? You gonna see if he'll check out your backyard?" my dad asked.

I smiled at him. "Yeah. Think I will."

29

Victor pointed the neck of his beer bottle at me. "You are actually becoming an investigator."

We were on my back deck, under the trellis, the grill warming, drinking beer. I'd called him when I left the fair after talking with my dad, told him what I'd learned, what I wanted to do and, surprisingly, he'd agreed to come over, as long as I provided some dinner and beer.

"I think that was a compliment," I said.

"I think it was, too." He glanced at the bottle. "I better not have any more or we'll be kissing."

"Kissing my knee, maybe."

He ignored my insult. "When's this guy supposed to get here?"

I glanced at my watch and sipped from the beer. "Any minute."

On cue, the doorbell chimed inside the house.

"Punctual," Victor said with a smirk. "Friggin' sales guys."

"Feel free to jump in if you think it's necessary," I said.

"Gee, thanks for your permission, Dick Tracy. You ain't *that* good yet. Don't let your empty head swell."

The glass slider slid open and a guy in his late twenties with slicked-back hair wearing a bright green polo shirt and khaki pants and an obnoxious smile stepped out in front of Julianne, who was munching on a giant pickle wrapped in aluminum foil.

"I'll scream for you if the kid falls out," she said in between bites, patting her belly.

"Perfect," I said, smiling at her.

She closed the slider and the guy's smile brightened even more. "What a great lady. You are very lucky."

I stood. "Yes, she is and yes, I am. I'm Deuce. And this is my friend, Victor."

"Corey Stewart," he said, shaking my hand enthusiastically. If he was taken aback by Victor's midgetness, he didn't show it, smiling just as broadly at him and extending his hand. "Corey Stewart."

Victor slid out of the chair and shook his hand. "Yeah. Hey."

Corey surveyed the backyard. "Man, this is a great layout. Love the deck and the trees are terrific. Bet your kid loves playing out here."

Victor rolled his eyes and slid back into his chair.

"Oh, thanks," I said, then gestured at the empty chair next to Victor. "Yeah, she does. Have a seat. Get you a beer?"

"Ah, can't, on the job, but thanks." He set down his leather shoulder bag and eased into the chair. "When's your wife due? Julianne, was it?"

"Yeah. About a week ago."

He chuckled. "Whoa. She wasn't kidding, then, about screaming, was she?"

"She rarely kids about anything."

"Well, I don't want to take up too much of your time, then," Corey said, setting his hands on his thighs. He smiled at Victor, who returned a fake smile. Corey looked back at me. "You said on the phone you were interested in a lease estimate and analysis."

"Right," I said. I wasn't, but he didn't need to know that quite yet.

He opened his bag, pulled out an iPad and started tapping away at it. "Mind if I walk the yard for a minute?"

"Have at it."

He hopped down the stairs and walked slowly along the fence line.

"Watch out," Victor whispered. "You're not careful, you'll end up buying a used Buick from him or something."

"He's pretty good," I whispered back.

"Salespeople always give me the creeps," he

said, frowning. "All that fake happiness and crap isn't good for anyone."

"He's just doing his job."

"Well, his job is lame."

Corey hopped back up on the deck and sat down again. He nodded at the yard and then smiled at me. "You live in a good spot."

"How's that?"

"Well, most of the Rose Petal area is built over shale rock, which is a tremendous source for natural gas," he explained, looking from me to Victor and then back to me. "Taitano Resources has made a commitment to help reduce energy costs by extracting as much natural gas as possible from the shale in order to help preserve other resources." He smiled at me. "And when you own land where shale is present beneath the surface, we feel obligated to compensate you more than fairly to use your land."

I doubted Corey or his company felt any obligation other than to make as much money as they possibly could, but I didn't say anything.

He tapped away at the iPad again. "Your entire property appears to rest on shale, so we'd be interested in exploring the entire subterranean area of your property."

"What exactly does that mean?"

He grinned. "You a baseball fan?"

"Sure."

"Favorite team?"

"San Diego," I said. "Makes no sense, but we

went on vacation there as a kid and my dad took me to a game there. Padres have been my team since then. Probably to spite my dad, who's a big Rangers fan."

Corey chuckled. "We might not be able to do business then. I'm a Dodgers fan."

"Ugh. Now I really don't trust you."

He laughed harder than was necessary. "Now, now. We can do this peacefully. But, in baseball parlance, your home is like a grand slam."

"How's that?"

He smiled again at me. "Well, it's a bit complicated. But the simplest way to explain it is that we do some digging, squirt a little water down there, and see what comes up. My guess is that a lot is going to come up. A grand slam." He tapped at the iPad, then spun it around and showed it to me. "And this is what we'd pay you to explore your land."

I started to say something, but then did a double take at the number on the screen. It was at least three times what I was expecting to see. I looked at Corey. He was smiling, having noticed the double take.

"Taitano Resources wants you to know that they appreciate your permission to use your property," he said, grinning. "Like I said, we know it's an inconvenience to temporarily turn your property over to us. We believe in repaying your generosity with fair financial payment."

No wonder my father was having trouble saying no. If my little suburban house and lot was worth the number Corey Stewart was showing me, I couldn't imagine the figure they'd given Dad.

"So, do you pay per acre?" Victor asked, glancing at me, annoyed that I'd gotten sort of lost in the dollar signs. "The bigger the plot, the bigger the dollar amount?"

"I guess that's one way to look at it," Corey said, nodding thoughtfully. "A larger parcel of land means more shale for Taitano Resources to explore, which means the owner of the land should be more compensated, as well. It all depends on what's below the ground, but in a shale-rich area like this? Absolutely, the bigger the plot, the bigger the dollar amount."

"So a huge hunk of land might bring in a pretty good haul?" Victor asked, raising an eyebrow.

Corey upped the wattage in his smile. "For sure. Are you the owner of a huge hunk of land, Victor? Because I'd love to come take a look at it, if you're interested in working with us."

Victor yawned and waved a hand at me. "Can we get on with this, please?"

Confusion settled on Corey's face, but he didn't lose the smile.

I handed Corey back his iPad. "I think the

huge hunk of land Victor is talking about is the Carriveau County fairgrounds."

The brilliant smile flickered. "I'm sorry?"

"I think we may have forgotten to mention this when you sat down," I said. "But Victor and I are business partners."

"In real estate?"

"No, in an investigations service. And we're looking into George Spellman's death."

The smile was now dimming by the second as he overplayed the confused expression. "Who is George Spellman?"

"The guy you knocked out at the fairgrounds a few weeks ago," I said.

And just like that, Corey Stewart's smile was gone.

30

"First," Corey Stewart said, pointing at me, "I don't appreciate being brought here under false pretenses."

Neither Victor nor I said anything.

"Two, that guy grabbed me and when he wouldn't let go, I pushed him and he smacked his own head on a rock on the way down," he said, looking back and forth between us. "He grabbed me first and wouldn't let go. I was defending myself more than anything."

I looked at Victor, but he was staring at Corey.

"And, three, I had no idea the guy was dead and if you're insinuating that I had something to do with his death," he said, his hand shaking a bit, "well, screw you."

"Nobody was insinuating anything," Victor said, frowning. "Just keep your pants on."

"I was told you punched George," I said.

"Well, that's crap," he said, his face pinching together. "I've never punched anybody in my life. He grabbed my arm, and he wouldn't let go. I told him like three times to let go and he wouldn't. I tried to shake free, but I couldn't. So I pushed him away. He tripped and fell backward and banged his head." He frowned. "Yeah, I left him there. But he was breathing, he was sort of mumbling, and he wasn't bleeding. He was fine. I didn't do anything to him."

"Why was he grabbing your arm?" I asked.

He shoved the iPad back in his bag. "He said I didn't belong there."

"Did you?"

He zipped up the bag with a flourish. "Look, man. I was just doing my job. I was surveying, mapping, and measuring. That was it. I had permission to be there, but that guy didn't believe me."

His story was different from the one Matilda had told me, but not completely. He was speaking pretty clearly and forcefully, though. Didn't seem like he was lying to me. I'd been fooled before, but he was coming off as pretty honest.

"Someone hired you to analyze the fairgrounds?" Victor asked. "To see if you guys could do your fracking thing there?"

He hesitated, then nodded. "Yeah."

"Who hired you?" I asked.

"I don't have to tell you that. I'm not required to divulge who I work with, to anyone."

"And I don't have to tell the local police I think you're lying, but I might," I said.

Victor grinned, clearly pleased at my interrogation technique.

Corey's cheeks flushed pink. "I'm not lying."

"I didn't say you were," I said. "I said I might tell the police I think you are, so they can kinda mess up your life a little. And maybe embarrass your company a little bit. That probably doesn't sound like fun, though, does it?"

His hands balled into fists on his khaki-covered thighs. "Okay. I was hired by the owner of the fairgrounds to explore the possibility of drilling on-site there."

"The county hired you?" I asked, raising an eyebrow.

"The county doesn't own the fairgrounds," Corey replied.

"Who does?"

"I don't have to tell you that."

Victor reached into his pocket and pulled out his cellphone. "You got another one of them business cards, Corey? I'd like to call your boss and let him know there might be an investigation that you're gonna be involved in."

Corey's cheeks flushed again and he ran a hand through his perfectly coiffed hair. He was contemplating cracking, but wasn't completely there yet.

We waited him out and the crack took hold.

"I'm not supposed to divulge this," he said.

"Our client asked for complete privacy and I said we would honor that."

Victor rolled his eyes. "Sure, sure, kid. Whatever. Who owns the fairgrounds? Or give me the card. Now."

Corey Stewart's mouth set in a grim line for a moment and resignation settled into his features. "A woman named Marjorie Biggs."

Aka Mama Biggs.

31

"Mama Biggs *owns* the fairgrounds?" I asked, not believing it even as I said it.

Corey Stewart stood, sensing that he'd delivered some very unexpected news. "I'm gonna go."

"Sit down, dude," Victor said, waving the phone at him. "We're not done yet."

Corey sighed and sat back down.

"She actually owns the fairgrounds?" I asked again. "You verified that?"

"Of course I verified it," Corey said, annoyed. "No way I'd spend all that time surveying a piece of land that size without making sure I was dealing with the owner."

"How long has she owned it?" I asked.

"No idea. I just needed to verify current ownership and she is the current, sole owner of all of that land that we are looking at."

"Did Spellman know that?" Victor asked. "Is that why you and he tangled?"

Corey shrugged. "Not that I know of. He never said a word about it and I sure as heck didn't say anything about it. He just wanted me to leave the grounds. But she'd given me permission to do the preliminary work. She just asked that I do it early in the morning before anyone got there." He shrugged again. "He wasn't supposed to be there."

That fell in line with what Matilda had told me. I wondered if she or George had just exaggerated what went down during George's confrontation with Corey. Corey was definitely miffed about talking to us, but I still didn't get the sense that he was lying to us about anything.

"So she is exploring the possibility of having you drill on the fairground land?" I asked.

He shook his head. "She's not exploring. It's a done deal."

"A done deal?"

"We signed the paperwork last week," Corey said, nodding, gaining some of his confidence back. "Biggest deal I've ever closed. Couple more like that and I'll be able to *buy* the Dodgers."

"So then what happens?" I asked.

"What do you mean?"

"Do you own the land? How does it work?"

He shook his head. "No, we lease the land, just like we would here. We explore. We drill. We get into the shale to harness the gas."

"For how long?"

"Every lease is different," he said. "Size of that land, lease will run for about two years. It takes a lot of time. Now, your property? Be more like six months."

Two years. Meaning the fair wouldn't be held there and she'd need another place to put it. Which explained her interest in the parcel of land my father told me about. It didn't tell us a whole lot about George Spellman, but it did answer some of my questions about the fair.

"So she hasn't sold it," I said, clarifying. "She's just giving you the right to drill on it."

"Yep. That's how it works."

"Does she get a share of the profits?"

"Nope. When you lease, you lease up front and give up your rights to anything we find on the property," Corey said. "That number that caught you off-guard? I wasn't kidding. It really is more than fair. But whatever we are able to take from beneath your property is ours after you lease the rights to us."

"Is the land usable during the process?"

"Depends," he said. "Here? Sure, your backyard would be okay. We'd use a small crew and it would be pretty unobtrusive. There would be days when it wouldn't be, but most of the time, it would be okay."

"Yeah, except for all the crap you'd drop into the water supply," Victor said, raising an eyebrow.

Corey rolled his eyes. "Our process is safe and environmentally sound."

"So was Chernobyl."

"That makes no sense."

Victor waved a small hand at him. "Whatever, Slick."

Corey turned his attention back to me. "So, here, it would be a minor inconvenience. But there? Our process will be pretty extensive due to the excessive amount of shale beneath the surface. It won't be usable until we're done with it."

"So the fair couldn't be held there next April?" I asked.

He shook his head. "No way. Nothing will be able to be held there. It'll be in full swing at that point. But she said she had a lead on another location." He shrugged. "Sounds like she's got it all figured out."

It sure did.

32

Victor waved a BBQ-slathered rib in the air. "This town is insane."

Julianne and Carly had already finished their food and were inside, getting Carly ready for their girls' night at the fair. Victor and I were polishing off the remainder of the ribs, hashing over our meeting with Corey Stewart.

"Tell me something I don't know," I said, finishing my last rib and the rest of my beer. "I've lived here my entire life."

"I mean, you guys are really nuts," he said, shaking his round head. "It's like Fantasyland crossed with Oz here."

I nodded. He wasn't entirely wrong. Rose Petal wouldn't have been Rose Petal without some sort of insane drama playing out.

"So here's my question," Victor said, wiping his hands on a napkin. "What exactly did George Spellman know?"

I thought for a moment. "The only thing we

know for sure is that he ran into Stewart on the fairgrounds that morning. That's the only certainty we have and, even with that, we have two different accounts."

"I believe the sales guy," Victor said, grabbing his beer. "Yeah, he's kind of a dipstick, but I think his story makes sense."

"Why?"

"If Spellman got punched, like the other broad said, wouldn't other people have noticed? Wouldn't there have been a black eye or something like that?"

That made sense. "I suppose."

"So I think this dude went to the fairgrounds to do his measuring or whatever it is he does, and Spellman surprised him. Spellman got all indignant about his being there, got a little handsy, and got knocked down," Victor said, drinking the beer, then setting the bottle down. "And I don't think Stewart told him squat about the land deal."

"Why not?"

"Because he doesn't seem the type," Victor answered. "That guy cares about one thing. Commission. No way he would've fouled up a big old deal like that by giving away details that he was supposed to keep to himself."

"But he just gave them away to us."

"Because we threatened him," Victor said with a smile. "And because we are scary and intimidating."

"Right."

"But Spellman could've easily made the jump,"

Victor continued. "A guy from that company, surveying the grounds. He could've put two and two together to figure out that something was cooking."

I pushed my plate away. "So maybe that's what he was talking about when he told that group that he knew something."

"Those tree-huggers? C.A.K.E.?"

"Yeah. He told them something was happening, that he needed to find out more. So maybe he has the fight with Stewart and realizes what's going on."

"And then he tells his girlfriend he went to the old bag, she tells him not to worry about it, he says he's going to go to the board meeting and make it public and—boom," Victor said, raising an eyebrow. "He's dead."

I nodded. It all fit together and definitely seemed connected. Somebody didn't want George letting people know about what was going down in Rose Petal. And it all sort of pointed squarely at one person.

33

"Find any more dead bodies?" Tom asked as he dealt the first hand.

After the ribs, Victor and I made plans to meet the following day at the fair. The girls headed off to their evening of fun and, as it was the last Friday of the month, that meant I was off to my monthly dorky dads poker night. Yes, it was fair week and everyone was busy, but some things were too important to mess with. The fact that each of us had quickly responded to Tom's e-mail, saying we were available, told me that everyone needed a night away from the fair and their families as much as I did.

"Not yet," I said, fanning through the cards he dealt me and frowning. "But I might kill *you* if these are the kind of cards I'm gonna see all night."

He chuckled.

"Do we have a plan in place in case your wife

decides to have the baby tonight?" Paul asked from across the table, his eyes on his cards.

"A plan?" I asked. "Yeah. I'll tear out of here and get her to the hospital."

Jeff rubbed his chin. "Hmm. We'll just hold onto your money, then, until you get back."

"Or, we could play for you," Brandon suggested, raising an eyebrow.

"I like that," Mark said. "That works. A chance for you to earn while you're gone."

"We'll use your winnings to buy the baby a gift," Raphael suggested as he tossed several chips into the middle of the table.

"Somehow, I think I might lose," I said. "So. No. My money goes with me."

"Chicken," Tom said.

"Cluck, cluck," I said. "Bet."

There was comfort in knowing that once a month, no matter what was going on in my life, I could jump out of the day and sit down with friends for cards, beer, crappy food, and friendly harassment. It was like I'd never left college and we'd never grown up.

"I heard your dad talking about an offer he got from the drilling business," Paul said, tossing several of his chips into the pile.

I nodded. "Yeah."

"He gonna take it?"

"I don't think so."

Tom raised an eyebrow. "No?"

I shook my head.

"I heard the money's good," he said.

"It is," I said. "But I don't think he wants them digging."

"Couldn't pay me enough," Brandon said, shaking his head and tossing his cards on the table. "It isn't safe."

Mark tossed his chips in. "Money is always safe."

"Not the money. The fracking."

Jeff made a face. "Oh, please. You're a hippy tree-hugger. It's perfectly safe."

"Tell me that after you have a three-headed baby," Brandon said, folding his arms across his chest.

"He's already been neutered," Tom said. "No chance of any-headed babies."

"I heard the remnants go right into the water tables," Raphael said, laying his cards down and folding. "Chemicals. Dirty water. Rock fragments."

Paul scowled. "Please. The process has been around forever and it's only gotten safer. It's safer than drilling for oil."

"How do you know?" Tom asked.

Paul's cheeks colored slightly.

I started laughing. "How much are they paying you?"

A number of catcalls and howls went up at the table.

"So, maybe I'm a little defensive," Paul said, chuckling. "But they are making it worth my while. That's all I'm gonna say."

Mark started laughing. "Me, too."

"You, too?" I asked.

He nodded. "I hate yard work anyway and with them digging in the backyard, I won't have to do squat for a while."

That discussion was a perfect representation of our group. We all had different political views. All had different views on education. On money. But none of us took any of it seriously enough to take offense. We could all disagree on different things.

As long as we were allowed to mock those we didn't agree with.

"So what exactly do they do?" Raphael asked. "Is it like in that movie with Bruce Willis where they take a massive drill to the moon?"

"Hardly," Paul said. "The way I understand it is they bring in some sort of drill and go down into the shale with some pressurized fluid. After it's located, they fire some water down into the shale to break it up, forcing the gas out, and they capture the gas and—boom! Gas prices go down."

"Yeah. Just like that," Brandon said, shaking his head.

"You know what I'm saying," Paul said. "They capture the gas and then do whatever it is they do with it. I'm not smart enough to understand that part."

"That part is fine," Brandon said. "It's what they do during and after. The gas can leak. The water tables can become contaminated. There's all sorts of bad crap that can happen."

Mark held up a finger. "*Might* happen. Not *will* happen."

"But they can't promise it won't," Brandon argued. "And the problem is, you don't know until well after the fact if it's happened. When the three-headed babies start popping up."

"But I'll be dead by then," Paul said, shrugging. "And I'll just tell my kids to go live somewhere else."

We all laughed at that, but I thought the discussion demonstrated the varied opinions on the subject and probably represented what was going on all over town. People were having to weigh the risks versus cashing a fat check. Given Julianne's staunch stance against it, there wasn't going to be a decision for me to make. But others were probably going to have to give some pretty good thought as to which way they wanted to go.

An hour later, I was down twenty bucks and two beers in.

"I wanna hear more about the dead body," Jeff said, munching on a jalapeño stuffed with cheddar. "What the hell exactly happened to that Spellman guy?"

"Wish I knew," I said. "But I really don't."

"I heard he and that Biggs woman were sleeping together," Mark said.

"Mama?" Paul asked, appalled at the idea.

"No, no," Mark said. "That daughter." He looked at me. "That right?"

"I'm not at liberty to discuss," I said.

"Please," he said, making a face. "You aren't a lawyer. You're a detective."

"Sort of," Tom said, grinning. "I still think of you as unemployed. I like it better that way."

I rolled my eyes. Some myths refused to die and the story that I simply couldn't find a job was a Rose Petal myth that would probably follow me forever. I knew he was kidding, but they all knew it drove me nuts.

"You can tell us," Raphael said. "We won't tell anyone."

"Except your wives, who will then spread it all over town like the flu," I said.

They all looked at one another.

"Excellent point," Brandon said. "You probably shouldn't tell us anything."

Mark leaned across the table. "They were totally doing it, weren't they?"

"Thanks for the image," Paul said, shutting his eyes, no doubt trying to erase said image from his mind.

"I'm not saying anything," I said, smiling at Mark. "Nada."

"You are no fun," he said, frowning. "The rest of us go to our crappy jobs every day, sit at the desk, staring at our computers. But you? You get to go eavesdrop and stalk people and do detective stuff."

Tom nodded. "It's true. We do live a little vicariously through you."

I looked at the useless cards in my hand and tossed them on the table, folding. "Then how about if you repay me with some decent cards?"

He pretended to think for a moment. "Never mind. I don't need to live vicariously through you. I'd rather have your money. Or, sorry, your wife's money."

That brought more than a few hoots and hollers and I stood to grab some more food that would contribute to my early death.

"You guys settle on a name for the baby?" Raphael asked.

"No," I said quickly. "Not yet."

Brandon glanced at me. "Why not? It's gonna be like any minute."

I shrugged, filling my plate with nachos and cookies.

"Yeah, why not?" Tom asked, smiling.

"Just haven't settled on one yet."

"Oh, that's weird," Paul said, staring at his cards. "I heard it was because you don't get a say in the matter."

The rest of them burst into laughs.

I chucked a cookie at the back of Paul's head. "Very funny."

"Julianne told Lynn," he said, still giggling. "Can't believe you don't get to name your own kid."

"Oh, shut up."

"But I guess that's the trade-off for getting to stay home," he said. "She pays the bills. She gets full naming rights."

All of them were giggling like third graders.

"Maybe you could get a cat," Tom suggested. "Maybe she'd let you name that."

The giggles turned to outright laughter.

"What about a fish?" Jeff asked.

"A hamster?" Mark offered.

"A bunny," Raphael said.

"A snake," Brandon said.

"I hate all of you," I said, throwing all of my chips at them.

But I didn't hate them at all. I appreciated the fact that, for one night every month, they would be there to pull me away from any crap I might be dealing with. And for the rest of the night, I didn't give a single thought to Mama or Matilda or George Spellman.

I just continued to lose money.

34

"You two better have something good for me," Mama Biggs said from her golf cart in front of the fair offices the next afternoon. "Because I've got a singing competition to run this evening and it doesn't just run itself."

I'd gotten home in the middle of the night, slept in late and enjoyed a lazy day around the house with Julianne and Carly. No baby yet, but everyone seemed to appreciate the quiet day at home before heading back to the fairgrounds.

Victor and I had driven over to the fairgrounds together, the girls to follow later on. He and I went through our conversation with Corey Stewart one more time. Everything pointed right at the person who had the most to gain from the deal, and the most to lose if the information about selling the fairgrounds got out.

"George Spellman knew about your deal with Taitano Resources," I said.

Mama Biggs was good. She caught herself before she could snap her face toward me, surprised.

"What are you talking about?" she asked, looking in my direction, but not exactly at me.

"We know you're leasing the fairgrounds," I said. "We know George came to you after seeing their rep on the fairgrounds. And I'm pretty sure you're looking at buying another parcel of land to move the fair to for the next couple of years. Which might all be legal and on the up and up, but it will anger a boatload of people here in Rose Petal. So you're waiting until after the fair to do it all quietly, when everyone is burnt out on fair news."

Mama stared at me and then at Victor, then moved her eyes back to me. "You're talking crazy."

"Look, lady," Victor said. "We know what we know. And right now, nothing looks good. You hired us to look into George Spellman's death, right? Well, as of right this second, everything points at you."

"At *me*?" she squawked, anger filling the lines in her forehead. "Me?"

We both nodded.

"So you two nitwits think I hired you both to look into a murder that I committed?" She rolled her eyes. "I think we got a pair of donkeys over in the barn that could've done better and come a lot cheaper."

She had a point about hiring us if she were the culprit, but she still owed us some answers. "First things first. Do you own these fairgrounds?"

She shifted in the golf cart, ripped the walkie-talkie off her belt, and twisted a dial on it. She set it on the seat next to her. "Fairgrounds are owned by my family, yes."

"The county doesn't own them?"

"Not for about twenty-five years," she answered, raising an eyebrow at me. "My daddy struck a deal back before Rose Petal was Rose Petal. He owned this land. Actually, he owned most of Rose Petal. But he sold most of it off and then managed to gamble all the proceeds away." She shook her head. "My mama and he used to really go at it."

The walkie-talkie crackled and she picked it up and turned another knob on it, laying it back down.

"Anyway, he held onto this land, for some reason," she continued. "But when the county incorporated in the fifties, they wanted a public use land. They wanted this spot. But Daddy owned it. So they worked out a deal." She smiled. "Daddy may have been a degenerate, but he was no dummy."

Victor sighed, his patience waning.

"He gave them the land for a small fee," she said. "The town didn't have much money back then and he did want to help it grow. So he basically gave it to them for nothing. He took a small cut of the fair revenue and of anything else that was held here. But the term was limited."

"Limited?" I asked.

She nodded, her tight gray curls bobbing up and down. "Yes, sir. Limited. Their ownership was more like a long-term rental. It was the county's to use for forty years. When that agreement expired, the land reverted back to my family. My daddy and my mama were gone by then. So it came back to me."

That sounded like it was probably true. A lot of Texas towns were started with handshake land agreements that eventually expired. A lot of them became public when they expired. But not all of them, apparently.

"So when it came back to me, I didn't make a big deal about it," she said, shrugging. "I didn't see the need to put the family name on the fairgrounds. It's still used by the county for everything it always was." A crooked smile formed on her face. "Revenue just goes to a different bank account."

"And now you're selling the land?" I asked.

"I'm not selling nothing," she said, narrowing her eyes at me.

"Leasing," Victor said, adjusting his hat.

Her hands clutched the steering wheel of the cart. "I suppose everyone's gonna find out soon enough. Yeah. I'm leasing it."

"To Taitano Resources," I said.

"They've offered me a small mint," she said, still smiling. "And I will still own the land when they are done with it."

"And you're going to buy the land up near Denton to move the fair to?" I asked.

The smile faded and she studied me. "I'm guessin' that daddy of yours is still tied to the bank and those bankers have big ol' mouths."

"Yes or no?"

She grabbed the walkie-talkie and set it in her lap. "You may be thinking some awful things about me right now, but you better know one thing. I wouldn't up and ditch the fair. It's been a part of my family for as long as I can remember. I know how important it is to the community and I would never do anything to harm it."

I glanced at Victor. His tiny arms were folded across his chest and he looked bored.

"So, yes, I am looking to move the fair," she said. "It's all in place. That new land is better plumbed, has better access, and can accommodate more exhibitors. It will actually be a better place to house the fair."

"It'll hurt Rose Petal," I said. "Local vendors and retailers will lose out on money that comes from people all over the county and the region."

"You don't think I know that?" she said sharply. "I'm well aware of that, Mr. Winters. I'll be doing what I can to accommodate them."

"How?"

"I don't know exactly and that's not your concern. But I will be taking care of the people here in Rose Petal. If I didn't, my daddy might up and rise out of his grave to tan my hide."

We stood there for a long minute. I was unsure what to say. I looked around and couldn't believe that everything was just going to be moved to a different place.

"Let's get back to the dead guy," Victor said. "He figured out what was going on, but you told him to shut up about it. Why?"

"Because it wasn't none of his danged business," she snapped. "And the paperwork wasn't all signed yet."

"When were you planning to tell everyone about the deal?" I asked.

"After the fair."

I thought back to Butch Dieter's questions at the board meeting and it clicked into place. "You were softening the blow."

She looked at me, annoyed. "Excuse me?"

"You were softening the blow," I said. "You were tweaking a few things this year. So you could spin it."

"What the heck are you talking about?" she asked.

Victor looked at me, too.

"The things that you've changed this year," I said. "You mentioned them at the meeting the other night. No demolition derby. The Ferris wheel has been broken. The horrific band." I paused. "You sabotaged this year's fair. You made sure there would be a few things wrong so that you'd have some justification for moving when you announce the move."

Mama's face reddened.

"And killing a guy in the 4-H food stand to

kill off the sales would give you even more justification," I said.

Mama pushed herself out of the cart, put her hands on her hips, and leaned closer to me.

"Listen here, Mr. Winters," she said, her mouth coiling up into a snarl. "I did *not* kill anyone. You wanna come after me for doing what I'm doing with my own land, fine. You wanna argue about where the fair's gonna be, fine. You wanna moan about the fact that you can't ride on the Ferris wheel, fine." She leaned in closer, so our noses were almost touching. "But I did not kill George Spellman. And you are an idiot for even considering it."

"I don't think it's that much of a leap to . . . ," I said.

"And I was well aware that my dimwit daughter was in love with George," she said, her mouth in full snarl now. "And no matter what I thought of that train wreck, I would not have killed the only man that has ever shown Matilda the least bit of kindness."

"So you knew," I said.

"Of course I knew," she snapped. "I'm not an idiot. And I knew how it would look if everyone knew about Matilda and George when they found him. So I told the board to distance themselves from him."

That would explain all of those weird statements about being *aware* of George.

"It was a mistake on my part," Mama said. "But that is all I've done."

"Well, I still think . . . " I said.

"Well, maybe you should stop thinking!" she said, cutting me off. "You think his death won't hang over this fair for years to come? No matter where it is, everyone is going to remember this. We'll always be the fair where they found a guy in the freezer. You think *that* won't cut into my bottom line next year? Or the year after?" She shook her head, frowning at me. "I'd be a fool to put a dead body anywhere on these grounds when I've got all my eggs in this basket." She squinted at me. "I'm gonna kill somebody, you better believe you'll never find that body."

She hopped back into the cart and slammed the accelerator to the floor, covering us in dirt and gravel as she sped away.

35

"She has a point," Victor said.

We were at the drinking fountain, rinsing the dirt from our mouths and faces from Mama's hasty exit.

"I guess," I said, shaking the water from my hands.

"No, she really does," Victor said, doing the same with his hands. "A dead body causes way more lasting damage than any of those other things. And now that she's admitted she's the owner, I think it makes less sense. She'd be hurting her own pocketbook. And then there's the whole hiring us thing. She may be a bit cracked, but she doesn't seem dumb."

No, Mama wasn't dumb. That was certain. And I agreed with Victor—given what we'd just confirmed with her, it seemed far less likely that she'd had anything to do with George Spellman's death. I could make a case that certain things pointed in her direction, but the financial part—which now seemed to be Mama's driving force—pointed the finger clearly away from her.

The problem was that I wasn't sure where it *was* pointing.

I stepped out from under the awning that housed the water fountain and into the late day sun. I was frustrated. I felt like we'd made no headway. And I wasn't getting to really enjoy the fair. I was too busy worrying about George Spellman, and about Mama's plans.

"So maybe this guy's death isn't related to her newfound business venture," Victor said, slipping his sunglasses from the brim of his hat to his face. "Maybe it was just bad luck and timing."

"Maybe."

"You said he was in some motorcycle group and that tree-hugger group," he said. "Maybe the answer is there somewhere."

"Maybe."

"Or maybe you could just keep saying maybe."

I squinted into the sun. "Maybe."

"Hey. Bozo. What's the matter?"

I shaded my eyes from the sun. The heat was intense. At least a hundred degrees. Too hot for April. Maybe that's what was frustrating me.

"I just find it hard to believe that all of this is going on and it's a coincidence," I said. "Could it be? Sure. But I'm just having a hard time buying that, particularly given the fact that he was somewhat involved."

"I wouldn't say he was involved," Victor said. "He seemed to have known about what was happening. But that doesn't mean he was involved."

"So, then, what? Someone killed him for another reason?"

"Sure. Happens all the time. Might not even be a reason. Might've just run into the wrong guy at the wrong time. It might not have been personal at all."

I sighed. He was right, of course. But I still wasn't buying the coincidence. George had his hands in too many things that were overlapping for me to buy that.

Victor looked at his watch. "I gotta scoot. Meeting the wife and kid for ice cream." He paused. "You should do the same."

"They'll be here soon," I said.

"No, I mean it, Deuce," he said. "You're wearing yourself out over this. Take a break tonight. It'll all still be here tomorrow. And maybe it'll make sense then."

I knew he was right. It was just hard to disengage sometimes.

"Spend some time with Julianne and your daughter," he said. "As soon as number two shows up, you're gonna be too busy to even think."

I laughed. "I know. And you're right. Thanks."

He tipped his hat as he started walking away. "You're welcome. And I'm always right, Stilts. Always."

36

Julianne and Carly arrived shortly after Victor left, and I was determined to take his words to heart. I felt like I'd been ignoring them and I wanted to rectify that. The fair had always been family time for us. With the closing of everything in town and Julianne always taking vacation days during that week, we usually spent it tethered together. I'd untethered myself and that didn't feel good. So I thought that night would be a good time to bond again.

During Carriveau County Idol.

Now, lots of fairs held their own singing competitions. Lots of fairs ripped off the singing shows from TV and tried to make them their own. But very few fairs put on a competition with the elaborateness that Carriveau County did.

There were town tryouts. Then town competitions early in the spring before fair week. Then all of the town winners were featured in the newspapers. A website was created. There were multiple age divisions. A local radio station hosted it. And then tickets were sold for the big night at the fair.

Mama was smart. She might have ditched the demolition derby, but she hadn't messed with CCI. There would've been an insurrection. It was the toughest ticket at the fair to get and something people talked about all year long.

Most of the singing was horrifically bad, but some of it was decent. Decent for a county singing competition, anyway. While the judges tallied up the final scores at the end of the evening, people were invited up to sing karaoke. And most of those who made it up on stage did so with the backing of a little—or a lot of—liquid courage.

We stopped to pick up a bright red slushy for Carly before working our way toward the stage. A long table was set up near the entrance, with a large plastic box on it.

"Daddy! A contest!" Carly pointed. "Can we enter?"

I glanced at the table. A trifold poster board advertised a weeklong getaway at some Texas resort.

I shrugged. "Sure."

She ran to the table and tore off an entry form. She thrust it and a pencil into my hand.

"Here. You fill it out and I'll drop it in the box."

I scribbled our name and address on it,

folded it in half, and handed it to her. She pushed it through the slot on the top of the box and came back beaming.

"I bet we win!" she said as she reached for her slushy.

We fled past the box and found our seats in the second row of bleachers, off to the side of the stage.

"We got good seats," Julianne said. "I'm impressed."

"Only the best for you."

"It was a lottery, wasn't it?"

"Yep."

"Well, at least we'll have an easy time getting out of here if your kid decides to enter the world this evening," she said.

"Win, win."

We were two contestants into the teenage division when someone tapped me on the shoulder.

I turned around to see Butch Dieter, the questioner from the board meeting. We shook hands.

"Haven't missed this in about fifteen years," he said with a grin.

"Me, either."

He shifted on the bleacher. "You make any headway on George's death?"

"Nothing to speak of, no, unfortunately."

He frowned. "Bummer."

"I did talk to Matilda, though."

He nodded solemnly. "Yeah, she's hurting pretty good. Feel bad for her." He paused.

"Sorry I couldn't tell you about her the other night."

"I understand," I said. "Rules are rules."

He nodded again. "Club is strict. But she was pretty good for him, you know?"

"How so?"

"He was kinda messed up for a while," Butch said. "Not in a bad way or anything, but I think he was lonely, kinda sad. He wasn't the same old George. He stopped telling jokes. Stopped showing up for the occasional beer. Just was withdrawn for a while. But when he started seeing her, the old George came back."

"Were they serious?"

Butch thought for a moment, then nodded. "I think so. They were kinda low-key about their relationship, but they seemed pretty serious, at least from what I knew about them."

I glanced at the stage. The MC was asking trivia questions to the people in the audience and tossing out T-shirts as rewards.

I turned back to Butch. "You said he was down for a while? How come?"

"Bad relationship," he said, shrugging. "Look, I know all the jokes people were probably making about Matilda because of her size, okay? But she was ninety times better for him than anyone else ever was."

Before I could ask any more questions, the music came up and the next singer started in on a horrific version of Journey's "Don't Stop Believin'."

Julianne leaned over so her mouth was right

next to my ear. "I used to love this song. Now I don't think I'll want to hear it ever again."

I smiled and nodded. "The sound of you screaming in labor will be more melodic than this."

And the rest of the evening was much of the same. Bad renditions of overly popular songs completely butchered by people who'd clearly been lied to about their talent. Julianne and I tried to contain our laughter by burying our faces on each other's shoulders. Carly just looked at us like we were weird.

Nearly two hours later, the sun had disappeared, replaced by the moon and temporary floodlights to illuminate the stage. Mosquitoes were out in full force and the judges were now set to begin their deliberations.

Which meant karaoke.

"You going up this year?" Julianne asked.

"Very funny."

She shifted on the bleacher next to me. "If I thought it would force the baby out, I'd go sing anything."

I put my hand on the small of her back and she released a small, grateful groan. I smiled at her and then took in the surprised look on her face. "What?"

She pointed at the stage.

Matilda had the mic in her hand and was working with the MC on the karaoke machine.

"Oh, my," I said, unsure I wanted to hear what might come out of her mouth.

Matilda pointed a finger at the screen and nodded firmly. The MC raised an eyebrow, shrugged, and punched a button on the keyboard.

Matilda strode to the middle of the stage, hitched up her black sweat pants, which were stretched to their absolute limits, and stared down at her feet, either preparing herself or studying the construction of the stage.

"Isn't this the song from *Titanic*?" Julianne whispered as the first notes floated out over the crowd. "Celine Dion?"

"'My Heart Will Go On,'" I said, nodding.

"Oh, my," Julianne said, clutching my arm, preparing herself.

Matilda's voice wavered with nervousness over the first few lyrics, then settled down, and I think everyone in the crowd was looking around at one another, wondering if they were all hearing the same thing.

Because she was pretty darned good.

Her confidence grew as she got deeper into the song, her eyes focused somewhere out beyond the crowd, her free hand sweeping out in a grand gesture over the people, bringing a fairly sizable round of applause as she continued on.

And that's when I noticed the tears coming from her eyes.

As the lyrics tumbled out of her, it seemed

pretty clear that she wasn't so much singing them as she was speaking them to someone else.

George Spellman.

She finished with a flourish and most of the audience rose to their feet, exploding with applause. Matilda wiped her eyes and handed the mic back to the MC, who was still encouraging the crowd to clap for her performance.

"Of all the things I've seen on this stage, that might've been the most surprising," Julianne said. "And touching."

I nodded in agreement as the applause finally started to die down. Not everyone in the audience was privy to the meaning behind the lyrics, but it was hard not to infer that the song meant something to Matilda. I could even hear Butch sniffling behind me.

As Matilda lumbered down the stairs from the stage, I noticed that her expression started to change. The sadness that had been draped all over her face was being slowly replaced by something else.

Anger. Or irritation. Or something along those lines.

And she was staring at Susan Blamunski, who was doing her best to return the stare.

"Wow," Julianne said, seeing what I was seeing. "*Rawr*, cat fight. Wonder what that's all about."

As Matilda reached the bottom stair, Susan met her there. They glared at one another and I couldn't be sure, but it looked as if Matilda bumped her with her massive hip as she passed. Susan tossed her another angry look over her shoulder as she went up the stairs to the stage.

"Maybe she took her song," Julianne said.

I nodded and watched as Susan marched up to the karaoke machine. She placed her hands on her hips, made an impatient face at the MC, and waited for him to pull up whatever she was looking for. When it was up, she grabbed the mic from his hand and marched to the middle of the stage, her face still masked with anger.

The first few notes of the song pulsated through the speakers and Julianne dug her nails into my arm. "Oh my God. Duran Duran? I used to love them!"

It was indeed Duran Duran and Susan plunged into a ferocious version of "Hungry Like the Wolf," prancing and preening around the stage in a near maniacal manner. She clawed at the air. She bared her teeth. Her singing was okay, but she was selling the act and the audience was eating it up, including Julianne, who was standing and singing along, one hand cradling her stomach, the other raised in full fist-pump mode.

Carly just stared at her mother, wide-eyed with wonder.

As the song wound down, Susan planted herself in the middle of the stage. She made one more clawing gesture at the audience and thrust the microphone into the air, an evil-looking smile settling on her face as she stared out into the wildly cheering crowd.

I followed her gaze.

Matilda Biggs was at the other end of it. She stood near the bleachers, her arms folded across her ample body, shaking her head, before she turned and walked off.

37

"It would've been awesome if they had just clawed each other's eyes out," Julianne said.

She was flat on her back in bed, her tank top pulled up to expose her enormous belly. I was next to her, my hand on the mountain, feeling for kicks or other signs that the progeny finally might want out.

"Susan doesn't seem the type to like Celine Dion," I said.

Julianne closed her eyes. "Maybe she's just into power ballads."

"Or maybe there was some sort of fair betting pool on who would win karaoke," I suggested.

"I totally would've participated in that pool."

We dissolved into laughter again. We'd had a good night. We'd had fun together. Fun had been missing from the fair until that night and I was glad it was back. Yes, Julianne was hot and miserable and I was frustrated. But there was comfort in the fact that we could still go out to something goofy and ridiculous like Carriveau County Idol and have a good time.

"Carly said she wants to sing next year in the kids' division," Julianne said, staring at the ceiling.

"Ummm . . . no."

"Why not?"

"Because she can't sing."

"She's a kid."

"Which is exactly how most of those other yellers ended up there in the first place," I said. "They didn't have a parent up there to tell them no."

"Why would you tell her no?"

"Because she *can't sing*. She unfortunately inherited my singing talent. Which means she got none."

Julianne frowned. "Hmm. I told her we'd see."

"You heard the way everyone mocked the people who got up there and couldn't sing," I said, rubbing her stomach. "You heard the way *we* mocked them. Do you want people doing that to our daughter?"

"They wouldn't mock her."

"Oh, yes, they would."

She thought for a moment. "I would kill anyone who mocked my child."

"Well, then, you'd have a long list to get through."

She laughed and tried to turn into me, but her stomach made it impossible and she groaned. "Oh my God. I'm going to rip this thing out with my bare hands if I have to. I can't even hug you."

I pulled her as close as I could and kissed her forehead. "Soon. It'll happen soon. I can feel it."

"There's no baby in you. You can't feel anything."

"Maybe I'm just intuitive."

"Maybe you're just saying things to try and make me feel better."

"Maybe."

She smiled and closed her eyes. "Well, that's okay, I guess." She paused. "I wanted to hug Matilda. I felt badly for her."

"I know. It was sad."

"I think she really loved George. The way she sang that song."

"Seemed that way."

She tilted her head so it was on my shoulder. "You need to find out what happened to him. For her."

I laid my hand over my heart. "I think I'm having a heart attack."

She opened her eyes. "What?"

"Are you actually asking me to do some investigating?" I said, still clutching at my chest. "You want me to stay on a case?"

She smacked me in the stomach. "Stop. I'm serious. I really wanted to hug Matilda tonight. She needs closure. She needs to know what happened to the love of her life. So figure it out. For her."

I took her hand from my stomach and kissed it. "Okay. I will."

"But do not miss the birth of your child or someone will have to solve your murder."

"You've been making a lot of death threats lately."

She closed her eyes. "All the more reason to do what I say."

38

Carly came into our room, yelling, "The parade's today! The parade's today!"

She was gone before I could groan at her about how early in the morning it was.

Julianne was still snoring softly, so I rolled myself out of bed and into the shower. I was downstairs twenty minutes later and Carly was already dressed and at the kitchen table.

"I'm excited," she said.

"Apparently so."

"You know I love the parade. And we get to march in it this year!"

"I'm aware."

"Aren't you excited, Daddy?"

I wasn't sure what I was. The forecast called for a temperature a degree or two over one hundred. I was already tired from a late night. Marching with the 4-H group in the parade in that kind of heat was not my idea of fun. But I knew she'd been looking forward to it for months.

"Yes, I'm excited," I said, sticking bread in the toaster for her and then pouring her a glass of milk.

The parade was the big finale for the fair. Yes, the rides on the midway stayed open until dusk, but the exhibit buildings would begin to empty, the vendors would begin folding up their tables, and the livestock owners would begin taking their animals home as soon as the parade ended.

Nearly every business in Rose Petal would have some sort of float, along with nearly every service organization within the county. Some would be as simple as a wagon with some marchers and some would be elaborate in their decoration. The 4-H one fell somewhere in between, having adopted the theme of "Come Grow With 4-H!" I hadn't seen it yet, but it had been described to me as an oversize garden on the back of a flatbed trailer.

The parade route was nearly a mile long, snaking down Main Street and finishing at the fairgrounds. The street would be lined with people on blankets and in lawn chairs, cheering and waving, as the marchers and float riders threw candy. A panel of judges would wait at the fire station, judging each float, working hard to determine who would win the hundred dollar check for that year, along with a small golden cup.

It was hokey, it was silly, and it was Rose Petal,

but it was ingrained in the DNA of the town and I'd been in it or at it every year of my life, and I wanted Carly to have those same memories as she got older.

I just didn't want it to be so hot.

Julianne found her way downstairs just as the toast popped up and I was scrambling eggs in the skillet. She glared at me with sleepy eyes, blaming me—again—for the fact that coffee was off-limits as long as the baby was inside of her. I pacified her with juice, the eggs, and some toast of her own.

Carly mowed through her breakfast and scrambled upstairs to change into her costume, which consisted of something that made her look like a human corncob.

Julianne pushed her plate away. "I was thinking about last night."

"You want to pursue a singing career?"

"Hardly. I mean, about Matilda and Susan. That whole look thing that was going on."

I slid the dishes into the sink. "Yeah?"

"I wonder if it was about more than the song choices."

"Why?"

She rolled her eyes. "Because I'm a woman. Because the more I thought about it, the more it felt like a bigger thing."

I filled the skillet with water to let it sit and loosen the egg skin stuck to it. "Okay. What kind of thing?"

Julianne stared longingly at my cup of coffee, then forced herself to look away. "Maybe Susan knows about the land deal. Maybe she's pissed about that. Or, maybe she's just blaming the entire Biggs family for screwing up her precious 4-H food stand."

I nodded and scrubbed the plates. "That could make sense."

"I mean, you know what that woman is like," Julianne said, and, even though I couldn't see her, I knew she was making a distasteful face. "She doesn't need a reason to be a pain in the rear end or to decide she doesn't like someone."

I chuckled. "Tell me how you really feel."

"You know it's true, Deuce," she said. "No, I can't stand her, but she just loves to create drama like she's still in high school. Every time I see her, she makes a snide comment about me. She did it the other day. She doesn't need a reason. And the only reason I'm telling you this is because I really do want you to help Matilda."

I shut off the faucet and dried my hands. "Her singing last night really got to you."

Julianne hesitated. "It did. I know I'm a big hormonal mess, but I felt terrible for her. And if someone is picking on her or making her life tougher than it already is, well, then, I guess I just want you to help her in any way you can. And if finding out what happened to her boyfriend is something that would help her, then you should do it."

"You're getting soft in your pregnancy," I said.

"You should shut up and be nice to me and not make fun of me, husband who is not carrying some alien life form that will not leave the mother ship."

"Duly noted."

"Now, I'm going to go upstairs and put on my hideous green T-shirt and pretend to be happy about marching in this parade in four-hundred-degree temperatures," she said, pushing herself up from the table.

"You're walking in the parade?" I asked. "I thought we agreed you'd ride on the float?"

"That was when I thought your offspring would arrive in a reasonable amount of time," she said. "Walking has been known to spur labor. I would walk to Oklahoma at this point, if I thought it would force this kid out of my stomach."

"You'll still be the most beautiful woman in the parade," I said. "Just like every other year."

"Oh my God, shut up," she yelled at me, going up the stairs. "If the kid's still in me, you'll get sex."

39

The 4-H float did not look like an oversize garden to me.

It looked like . . . something else.

The floats were all parked at the south end of Main Street, each group having been assigned a numbered slot in which to park their float and make last-minute adjustments and finishes. People were scurrying around, yelling at one another, yelling for tape and staples and extra hands.

We'd been assigned slot 27, so we were about middle of the pack. As we walked up to the float, Julianne and I in our green shirts, Carly in her tiny corncob outfit, I slowed when we got closer.

"What the hell is that?" I whispered to Julianne.

"I have . . . no idea."

I was glad I wasn't the only one confused.

Behind the white pickup truck was a flatbed

trailer. On the flatbed trailer were six long . . . things. Three green, three orange. I knew that they were probably supposed to be cucumbers and carrots, but they looked distinctly like . . .

"Don't even say it," Julianne whispered. "I can see it in your eyes. Do not say it."

"But they look like big, giant . . ."

"Vegetables," Julianne said. "They look like vegetables. Get your mind out of the gutter."

"I can't be the only one that sees this," I said. "Who the hell was in charge of the float?"

Julianne grinned at me. "Our pal. Susan."

"And she couldn't see that it looks like they have six big . . ."

"*Vegetables,*" Julianne said, emphasizing the word. "They are vegetables."

"Telling you right now," I said, pointing at the *vegetables.* "The judges are going to dock our float for being inappropriate."

"Well, take it up with the queen bee," Julianne said. "Because here she comes."

I looked to my right and Susan Blamunski was headed our way, a big fake smile plastered on her face.

"Doesn't it look fabulous?" she gushed, then eyed Julianne. "I know this is your first look at it, since you haven't been to any of our float decorating sessions."

"We were at the first two," Julianne said. "But I don't think you were."

Susan's smile flickered. "I don't recall that."

"Of course you don't," Julianne said. "I'm gonna go help Carly get situated."

"She's a bit touchy," Susan said, once Julianne was out of earshot. "Probably the pregnancy. And the extra weight."

"Saw you at Idol last night," I said, changing the subject.

"Oh, thanks!" she said, mistakenly assuming I was complimenting her performance. "I rehearsed for a couple of weeks."

"I take it you and Matilda aren't friends?"

She raised a thin eyebrow at me. "Why would you think that?"

"Just seemed like there was something between the two of you."

She fumbled with a square of tissue paper and started folding it accordion-style. "Oh, I think she's just going through a tough time right now. I feel badly for her. But I like Matilda just fine." The fake smile reappeared. "I need to go pomp that one cucumber."

"Pomp?"

She held up the tissue paper. "You stick this in the chicken wire." She smiled. "Pomping."

"Ah. Got it."

She hustled off to pomp the . . . cucumber.

I stood around, looking for something to do, but everything seemed to be covered, so I wandered down the sidewalk to the group in front of us.

And ran into Dorothy.

She seemed startled at first, then just nodded as if she'd expected to run into me. "Oh. Hi."

"Hey."

She peered around me. "Interesting float."

"I had nothing to do with it." I looked past her. A group of about twenty people surrounded a simple pickup truck with a massive papier-mâché structure, which looked like the earth, in the back of it. They were all wearing bright orange shirts with "C.A.K.E." emblazoned across the front and a picture of Earth on the back. "I like the earth," I said.

"So do we," she said. "That's why we do what we do. The planet is in danger."

"I meant the one in the back of the truck."

She looked at me, puzzled, then shrugged. "Oh. Right. Yeah, it's pretty cool."

Scarecrow approached us, looking at me nervously. "What's going on?"

"I was just admiring your float," I said.

He looked at Dorothy. "Everything cool?"

She nodded but didn't say anything.

"Relax," I said. "The cops aren't going to jump out of the bushes."

They both glanced at the hedges for a long moment.

"You were right about George," I said. "He did know some things."

Scarecrow nodded and Dorothy muttered, "Told you."

"And he was going to do the right thing," I said. "At least, I think he was. But I just thought you both should know that."

They looked at each other, unsure what to

say. They shuffled their feet and looked around for a moment.

"We miss George," Dorothy finally said. "We're going to make him proud."

"Make him proud?"

She pursed her lips and both of them began backing up toward their float.

"You'll see," she said. "You'll see."

40

The roar of motorcycles filled the air behind the 4-H float and it took me a moment to realize it was the Petal Dawgs in the ready stall behind ours. I walked past our float and Butch waved a hand at me from atop his massive bike.

He flipped up his goggles. "Hey, Deuce. Looks like we're following you today."

"Looks like it."

"We'll try not to run you over," he said, chuckling. Then he gestured at the float. "Those things on your float? They look like . . ."

"Cucumbers," I said. "They're cucumbers and carrots."

He stared for a long moment. "Ohhhhhhh. Okay. Sure."

A clattering and scraping drew our attention to the other side of the street. A motorcycle was on its side and a guy was squirming beneath it like a trapped snake.

"Be right back," Butch said, jumping off his

bike, jamming the stand down, and hustling over to help.

A group gathered around the trapped man and helped to lift the bike off of him. He stood and brushed off his jeans, looking embarrassed. He adjusted the bright red bandanna on his head, tugged on the leather vest with the dog paw on the back and nodded all around.

Butch walked back over. "Some of these guys, the bikes are still new to them."

"You don't say."

"Archie there, the guy that took the spill, he's a doctor over in Argyle," he said. "He bought the bike a few months ago, but hasn't been able to ride it much. He's usually in surgery when we go out riding."

"Unlucky."

"We encourage everyone to take safety courses, but sometimes they don't have the time," Butch said, frowning. "And some of these guys, they just don't understand how heavy these things can be."

"You've had yours awhile?"

"Oh, I've been riding since I was a kid," he said, smiling. "My pop was a mechanic and used to buy 'em, fix 'em up, and sell 'em. I'd take 'em on test runs before we gave 'em back. One of the reasons I became an accountant was so I'd have enough money to indulge." He patted the bike. "I've got a couple more at home in the garage."

"Cool," I said. "I've never ridden."

"I'd be happy to take you out if you're ever interested," he said. "Of course, not on a group ride. That's against the rules."

I looked around at the Petal Dawgs. They were white collar guys living out their weekend fantasies. Most of them moved awkwardly around their bikes, more comfortable looking at them and showing them off than actually sitting on them.

"Maybe," I said. "Thanks for the offer." I gestured at his group. "You mentioned the other night that you were planning something? In George's honor?"

Butch's face grew serious. "Right. We are."

"Can I ask what it is?"

"Sorry. It's a surprise," he said. "Nothing disruptive. But we want everyone to remember George."

"Fair enough," I said.

"You learn anything new?"

I thought for a moment. "I think I've got some pieces of the puzzle. Just not sure how they all fit together."

He lowered his head. "You need any muscle, you can count on us."

"Muscle?"

"Yeah, muscle. In getting whoever did that to George." He took a look around at his fellow members. "We've vowed to not rest until his killer is brought to justice. Legally or illegally."

Behind him, Archie's bike started to tip

again and several others wearing the same vests helped him keep it upright. I was not looking forward to seeing him attempt to ride it and hoped we could keep at a safe distance.

"Thanks," I said. "But I think we've got it covered."

He fixed me with a hard stare, then nodded. "You can call on us if you need to. Offer will always be there."

Before I could respond, someone from near the 4-H float was calling my name.

I turned to see Susan waving at me.

"I need someone tall," she said. "Can you come over here for a moment?"

"Yep, one second," I said.

I turned back to Butch and his expression had changed. He looked as if he'd swallowed a lemon. Several of them.

"You know her?" he asked.

"Who? Susan?"

He nodded.

"She's our 4-H leader."

"I'd find a new 4-H group if I were you," he said, narrowing his eyes. "That woman is a menace."

"My wife feels the same way," I said, smiling. "We aren't her biggest fans."

"I'm serious," he said. "That woman ever steps in front of my bike, I'm hitting the throttle and I'll keep on riding."

"Bad experience with her?" I asked.

He rolled his eyes. "I wanted to throw tomatoes at her last night, Deuce. With pieces of glass in them."

"Sounds bad."

"She's the worst kind of woman," he said. "Controlling. Manipulative. Fake. Ugly."

I was surprised at his vitriol and I wasn't sure how to respond. I didn't know Susan well enough to confirm any of those things, but I didn't have a hard time believing they were true. Susan was a pain in the rear. Julianne wasn't the only one in town who couldn't stand her. I just hadn't known that Butch was in that line, too.

"Poison," Butch continued. "She's just poison."

"You used to date her or something?" I asked, curiosity finally getting the better of me.

He frowned at me like I'd spit on him. "Hell no. I'd never date that viper."

"Oh, sorry. It just sounded like you were talking from experience," I said, backtracking.

He shook his head. "No way. Not ever." He sighed. "We tried to get him away from her. But he had the hardest time cutting her loose. I think she just guilted the crap out of him."

"Who? A friend? Someone in the Petal Dawgs?"

"Remember when I told you George was way better off with Matilda?"

"Yeah."

"Never mind, Deuce!" Susan yelled. "We got it since you were taking so long!"

Butch shook his head and narrowed his eyes. "Susan was the one that broke George."

I blinked several times. "Susan and George? Used to be together?"

He nodded solemnly. "Until he finally got his head screwed on right and dumped her butt."

41

"I have to call Victor," I whispered to Julianne.

"So call him," she said, sitting on the edge of the flatbed. "And why are you whispering?"

I pulled my cell from my pocket. "I don't know."

"Well, don't. It's creepy."

I started to say something, but Susan materialized next to us. "Problem?"

I fumbled with my phone. "What? No. Why?"

She glanced at Julianne sitting on the flatbed. "I saw you sitting. Wondered if maybe you were going to have to leave. Maybe the heat was getting to you or something." She smiled.

Julianne smiled back. "I'm fine, Susan. But thanks for your concern."

"We have extra water bottles," she said. "And I could probably arrange for a wheelchair."

It was like I could hear the talons spring from Julianne's fingers. "Only if you think you might need one, Susan."

Susan tried to smile, but her face just scrunched up. "Oh, I'm fine. Okay. Toodle-oo."

She scurried around the back of the trailer.

Julianne looked at me. "What is the matter with you? You looked like you saw a ghost when she came around the corner."

"Did you know Susan and George used to be together?" I asked, lowering my voice again.

"George Spellman? The dead guy?"

"Yeah."

"No." She thought for a moment. "Well, that explains those looks Susan and Matilda exchanged last night."

"Yeah, it does."

Julianne rubbed her stomach and shifted on the trailer. "I would've yelled louder for Matilda last night if I'd known that."

"I gotta call Victor," I said.

She started to say something, but her words caught and she rubbed her stomach.

I held the phone in my hand. "What's the matter?"

She rolled her eyes. "I think I've overdone it on all the junk food and spicy stuff. My stomach feels rotten."

"You wanna go home?"

She frowned at me. "Uh, no. I won't give that woman the pleasure of leaving."

"Jules. Be real here. If you don't feel great, the last thing you should be doing is riding a float in a parade in this heat," I said.

"I'm fine," she said, rubbing her belly. "I just need to burp or something."

"You are so sexy."

"Shut up."

"We'll be moving soon!" Susan called out from the sidewalk. "Everyone please be ready!"

Julianne pushed herself off the trailer. "You better call Victor now. I don't think she'll be happy about you using a phone in the middle of the parade. I gotta go find Carly and make sure she doesn't get run over." She waddled around the back end of the trailer.

I punched in Victor's number, but got his voice mail. I left him a quick message and told him to call me back immediately. I shoved the phone back in my pocket.

I could see some of the floats ahead of us moving. The C.A.K.E. people were assembling in front of us and the Petal Dawgs were warming up their engines and trying to stay upright behind us.

Susan was at the front of the float, getting kids in place and prancing around.

I hoped she wouldn't mind me walking near her in the parade.

42

The floats all started crawling forward. Half of the kids were on the float, the other half walking in the street, armed with bags of candy to toss to the people lining the route The adults were interspersed throughout, keeping the kids in line and making sure they weren't eating all the candy that was meant for the spectators.

Susan was walking off to the side, in a spot where she could supervise everyone. I sidled up next to her.

She smiled at me. "Is your wife still here, Deuce, or did she give up?"

"Still here," I said. "She's on the other side with Carly."

She glanced over the float, as if she didn't believe me. "Ah, yes. She's hard to miss, isn't she?"

"Yes, easily the most beautiful woman on

the parade route," I said, growing tired of her remarks about Julianne.

Apparently, my frustration was evident in my words, as Susan replied, "Absolutely, she is! Pregnant women have that glow, don't they?"

"Yes."

"Or maybe that's a sunburn," she said, grinning at me, her words meant as a joke.

"Right," I said. "Hey, I didn't know that you knew George Spellman so well."

Her grin flickered. "What?"

I'd wanted to wait to hear from Victor. I was always unsure of myself when I was starting to put things together and, as much as I didn't like to admit it, I sometimes needed his input to tell me if I was doing the right thing or not. But he hadn't answered his phone, Susan was making fun of my wife, and I was irritated.

"George? Spellman?" I said. "I didn't know you knew him so well."

She moved her eyes about, scanning the 4-H'ers as we walked. "Where did you hear that?"

"You used to date him?" I asked, ignoring her question.

"Oh, well, that was . . . I don't know. Ages ago, I think I'd say."

"Was it? Way I heard it, it wasn't that long ago."

Her smile was fading by the second. "Opinions vary, I suppose."

"So you did used to date him, though, right?"

She hesitated, then nodded. "Yes, we dated."

"For a long time?"

"I honestly don't remember," she said, shooting me a smile that contained more glare than smile.

"You don't remember dating him? Or you don't remember how long?"

"Deuce, I really need to focus on the parade," she said. "And I'm not sure why my dating life is any concern of yours. Unless, of course, you're looking . . ." She gave me what I guessed was supposed to be a flirtatious smile.

"I assure you I am not looking, Susan," I said. "I haven't looked at anyone but Julianne since the day I laid eyes on her. But I don't think it's too much to ask you to walk and talk at the same time. Is it?"

She didn't answer.

The entire parade line was still crawling. I knew it would take awhile for us to get moving at a true walking speed. I glanced over the float. Julianne was walking with Carly, holding her hand, but she had a weird expression on her face. Almost a grimace. I really wished she wouldn't push herself just to make a point to everyone else in the world.

"About six months," Susan said. "We dated for about six months."

"Was it serious?"

"Why are you being so nosy?"

"Because it's sort of my job," I replied. "I'm trying to find out what happened to him, so I need to find out more about him. Who his friends were. What was going on in his life. I didn't realize you had a relationship with him or I would've asked you about him sooner."

She nodded, accepting that that made sense. "I guess it was serious. I mean, we weren't going to get married or anything, but we were . . . together."

"How'd you meet?"

"Actually, here at the fairgrounds," she said, still refusing to make eye contact with me. "I don't remember exactly how, but I think I was here for a 4-H activity and he was here because he was always here. I probably needed something fixed in the food stand."

The pace of the parade started to increase just a bit and we were actually walking at nearly a full, comfortable stride now.

"He asked me out," she said, glancing at me. "He was very flattering. I couldn't say no."

"And you said yes? Right away?"

"Yes. I did. I thought he was nice. Somewhat handsome. I wasn't involved with anyone. And he had a good sense of humor. I like that in a man."

"So why'd you break up?"

Her face bunched up. "I'm not sure how that's any of your business, Deuce. I'm really not."

"Just trying to get a clearer picture of what went on in George's life."

She frowned, irritated or angry or something. "But it was ages ago."

"Well, not really." I paused. "And I saw the look you gave Matilda last night, so it seems . . ."

"You can just leave that heifer out of this,"

she said sharply. "I have nothing to say about that cow."

"Not a friend?"

She looked like she wanted to vomit. "Hardly."

"How come?"

Her eyes narrowed to tiny, angry slits. "Because she took George from me."

43

We were walking at an easy pace and I asked, "She took him from you?"

She nodded curtly. "Damn right she did."

"How?"

"Oh, you'd have to ask *her*," she said. "I'm not sure exactly what she offered him, but it had to be something."

"Why did it have to be something?"

She looked at me like I was crazy. "Look at me and look at her. Please."

Right then, I wasn't seeing anything that was attractive about Susan. The looks that had taken place between the two women the previous evening, however, now made perfect sense.

"So he broke up with you?" I said.

"Well, I don't know that I'd say that," she said quickly. "It ended up being mutual. I knew he was no longer interested in our relationship. Honestly, I was getting tired of him, too. I realized he was a bit too simple for me."

She wasn't making sense. She was contradicting herself. Not something that was working in her favor.

"So what happened when you broke up?" I asked.

"What do you mean?"

"Was it friendly? Ugly? How did it happen?"

She took a moment to look around and survey her troops. "I really don't see how any of this is helpful and I really don't appreciate you being so intrusive."

I nodded. "Okay. I'm sorry. You're right. None of my business. You won't mind if I go ahead and let the police know that I've talked to you, though, right?"

She flinched and her entire façade crumbled for a moment. Her pace slowed and she went from looking like someone who was supervising a parade to someone who was about to panic. She was not a good poker player.

"Well, I don't see why you'd need to do that," she said.

"Just to share information," I said. "Be cooperative with them. Maybe they won't even be interested. I don't know. But I do have a question for you."

She raised a perfectly manicured eyebrow at me.

"I saw you the morning he was found. You were there," I said.

She nodded slowly.

"You weren't upset," I said.

"I was, too," she said, lifting her chin.

"Yeah, about the effect on the food stand," I said. "How 4-H would take a hit financially. Not about George. And I find that very odd, considering that you had been in a six-month relationship with him."

"Oh, I don't think that's accurate," she said. "I don't think you know me well enough to know how I react when I'm upset about something."

"Well, Matilda was there and, even though I didn't know they were a couple, she was upset. I could tell that, then, about her."

"Maybe she'd just stepped on a scale," Susan said, frowning. "Or forgotten her lunch."

I didn't think that Susan's bitterness was solely because she was a nasty person. That certainly played into it, but I thought there was more behind her snarky comments.

"But I *was* upset," Susan said. "I had to keep my cool, though. For 4-H."

"Right," I said. "So why'd you tell me about George and Matilda then?"

Her face colored and she dropped her sunglasses from the top of her head to her eyes. "I thought that might be valuable information for you. Like you said. You need a clear picture."

"Or did you want me to think she had something to do with his death?" I asked.

Her mouth twisted like a pretzel. “Maybe she did.”

“She didn’t.”

Susan turned and walked backward for a moment, keeping her eyes on the 4-H marchers behind us. “You know that for sure?”

“Yeah, pretty sure.”

“She have some sort of alibi or something?”

“Or something.” Technically, Matilda didn’t have an alibi. But she’d convinced me that she wasn’t capable of killing the man she loved. And I didn’t think that was any of Susan’s business.

“Do you?” I asked.

“Do I what?”

“Have an alibi?”

She turned around so she was walking forward again. “Of course.”

“Okay. What were you doing?”

We continued walking, but she didn’t say anything.

“Susan.”

She looked at me. “What?”

“Your alibi. What is it?”

She ran a hand through her hair, smoothing it down. “We’re getting close to the judges’ stand. I need to make sure we’re ready. We do not want to blow this opportunity in front of the judges. We have an excellent chance to win the float competition this year, I think.”

“We’ve got a few minutes,” I said.

She stopped abruptly and jammed her hands on her hips. “Deuce Winters, I am trying to coordinate this event and I don't appreciate getting the third degree from you right now. I'll be happy to talk to you at the end of the parade. But right now I have a group to organize so we don't look like fools in front of the judges."

She stomped off to the front of our float.

44

Main Street was lined with people and lawn chairs and pets and signs. The denizens of Rose Petal lived for the fair parade and despite the ungodly heat, they had turned out in full force to line the route, cheer for the floats, and collect candy.

I was struck for a moment that all of this was going to change. The parade would be elsewhere next year. And the year after that. Would it ever come back? Maybe. But for the next couple of years, the parade would be different and the people lining the streets would be different. The folks who lived in the tiny houses on Main Street and set their lawn chairs at the curb wouldn't be able to do so anymore. Would they travel to the new site and find spots on the new parade route? Or would they just let it go, disappointed that the tradition was gone? It made me sad for them and for the town.

I'd let Susan go and had moved over to the other side of the float with Julianne and Carly. Carly was busy tossing candy and Julianne was busy trying not to get sick.

"What were you talking to Susan about?" she asked with a grimace.

"Don't worry about it," I said. "But I think we need to get you home."

"I'm fine."

"No, you're not. You look like you're about to throw up."

Her face was flushed and sweat was pouring down her cheeks. Her walking was labored and I could tell that the heat had swelled her ankles to twice their size. She was breathing hard and every few steps she'd cringe.

"Well, if I do, just step out of the way and keep walking," she said, forcing a smile.

"It's too hot out here for you. Come on. This is ridiculous."

"Deuce, I'm not leaving," she said, glaring at me. "I refuse to play the delicate pregnant woman here."

"No one thinks you are."

"Exactly. All the more reason for me not to play it."

Her stubbornness could be incredible at times. "If you pass out, should I just put you on the float?"

"I'm not going to pass out."

"I just want to be prepared. If you won't go

home, I feel like I need to be prepared for any possible scenario."

We turned a corner and the judges' tower near the fire station was in view. The cheers were getting louder as each float passed by and did its best to impress Mama and her gang on the tower. Everyone liked to play down the importance of the parade, but there was no mistaking it. Winning the parade was the crowning achievement of fair week, and allowed the winners to brag for a year. It mattered.

"Yes, just put me on the float," Julianne said, then winced. "But not near the penises."

"Cucumbers."

"Whatever."

I shook my head. If I saw anyone else looking the way she did, I would've called paramedics. Such an incredibly stubborn woman.

I moved away from her so I couldn't choke her. I could see the C.A.K.E. people ahead of us scrambling to get in place for their pass at the judges. Something didn't look right, though. They weren't smiling or having fun.

They looked nervous.

I moved back next to Julianne. "Listen. Something may happen here in front of us."

She arched an eyebrow. "Those weirdos in the neon shirts?"

I nodded. "I'm not sure what, but I think they've got something planned."

"Like a dance or something?" she said. "They can't hold up the line. Everyone will freak."

"Not a dance," I said. "But something else. And if it goes a little nuts, we're leaving."

"I already told you, I'm not . . ."

"Jules, I love you," I said, taking her by the elbow. "But shut up. I'm done with the stubbornness for today. You look like hell and if anything goes weird up here, we're leaving and you are going home and getting in bed and that is the end of that. I will throw your pregnant rear end over my shoulder and carry you out of here if I have to. So just stop. Got it?"

She stared at me, her mouth open, like she couldn't believe I'd just told her to shut up. I was kind of pleased with the fact that I'd left her speechless. Of course, given the fact that she was nearly ten months' pregnant, I knew there was no possibility of her catching me if I had to run from her.

She started to say something, but stopped, then shook her head.

"Thank you for not arguing," I said.

"The only reason I'm not arguing is because I think I just had a contraction," she said.

45

"Are you serious?" I asked.

"Don't I look serious?" she said, her teeth clenched. "I'm covered in sweat and grabbing my stomach. Yes. I'm serious."

"You've been grabbing your stomach and sweating since we got here."

"I can still punch you."

"I'll get Carly," I said. "We need to go."

"You'll do nothing," she said, glaring at me. "I'm going to time them and we're going to keep walking. I'm going to make sure this little beast is coming out for sure before I go anywhere. I don't trust it. Would be just like this kid to try and fake me out. It's a little liar. So we are gonna wait."

"Jules."

"Now it's your turn to shut up," she said, smiling at me. "And check your watch. I'll let you know when the next one arrives. The only thing you're gonna do is count."

This was the problem with marrying a mule-stubborn woman.

I sighed and marked the time on my watch. The C.A.K.E. people were mobilizing in front of us as we approached the judges' tower. Scarecrow was on the float standing next to the "Earth," looking like he'd stolen something. Dorothy was walking next to the truck, her hand pressed to her ear. I squinted and could see a small Bluetooth receiver in her ear.

Odd.

Two other guys were on the float next to Scarecrow and they looked just as nervous. Other members of C.A.K.E. were flanking each side of the float, moving like they were the Secret Service, scanning the crowds on the sidewalk. I couldn't tell if they were actually looking for something specific or if they were just keeping watch.

Their float began to slow as they approached the judges' tower. I could see Mama up on the tower, under her umbrella, a clipboard on her lap, her expression hidden behind a large pair of sunglasses. Bruce was next to her, looking bored. Matilda was next to him, trying to smile and wave, but she didn't seem too into it.

The C.A.K.E. truck stopped and I could see Dorothy's lips moving, but she didn't seem to be talking to anyone near her. Clearly, the Bluetooth was in her ear for a reason.

Scarecrow shuffled around the Earth and put his hands on the paper-mâché orb.

And then lifted off the top of the Earth.

"Oh, crap," I said. "Here we go."

"Number two," Julianne said through gritted teeth and bent slightly at the waist. "That was like almost fifteen minutes, right? We're totally fine."

I glanced at my watch. "Yeah. Fourteen minutes."

She took several quick breaths, then made an undistinguishable sound that was somewhere between a squeal and a grunt.

"No problem," she said, her hand still resting on her stomach, but trying to straighten her posture. "I'm good."

I moved my eyes back to the Earth. The top was now on the flatbed next to the planet and several more members of C.A.K.E. had popped out of it.

With thick firefighter hoses.

"This is what fracking feels like!" Dorothy suddenly yelled.

Matilda and Bruce looked confused, but Mama looked pissed that anyone had the nerve to do anything out of the ordinary at her parade. She leaned forward in her seat, mouth open, about to yell something at them.

And then she looked wet.

The Earth, in addition to containing people, was also filled with some sort of water container, because the hoses were spraying the judges. Long, heavy streams of water crashed all over Mama, Bruce, and Matilda.

And the C.A.K.E. members were now chanting "NO FRACKING!"

The crowd was screaming; people were running around, unsure as to whether this was part of the show or it was something they needed to be worried about.

And, off to the side, I saw Susan Blamunski sneaking down the sidewalk, trying to disappear in the chaos.

I knew it. I knew she had something to do with George's death and I'd spooked her. There was no way I was letting her get away.

"Uh-oh," Julianne said. "This isn't good."

"I told you something was happening. I can't figure out how they filled that thing with water. There must be a tank of some sort."

"No," she said. "Not what I mean, Deuce."

I looked at her. Her hand was still on her stomach, but her breathing had slowed and her jaw didn't look like it was clenched shut. But she was standing in a large puddle of . . . something.

"My water just broke."

And then it really got crazy.

46

"Your what just what?" I said amid the shouting and noise.

"Relax," she said, leaning against our now stationary float. "My water broke. The beast is definitely coming." She pumped a fist in the air. "Yes!"

I glanced away from her. Susan was making her way up the sidewalk, moving into the thicker part of the crowd, looking back over her shoulder. I didn't want her to get away.

"We have some time?" I asked.

"Yeah, we can finish the parade," she said, then looked at the chaos in front of us. "If there is a rest of the parade."

The C.A.K.E. protesters were still firing water at the judges and screaming, but people were realizing that it wasn't part of the show and were starting to flow from the street to their truck to try and stop them. Mama, Bruce, and Matilda were trying to scramble down from their now soaked stage on the tower, but the hoses were making it difficult. Several men from the crowd were climbing aboard the C.A.K.E. truck and wrestling with Scarecrow and his cohorts. Dorothy was still screaming her brains out.

And Susan was getting away.

"I need to go get Susan," I said.

"What?"

"I can't explain now," I said. "But she's trying to escape."

"From *what*?"

"I think she killed George! And she's running!"

"Deuce, so help me, if you are chasing that woman and miss . . ."

"I won't. I promise."

". . . I swear to the Lord, I will murder both you and Victor and I'll tell this child that he or she was immaculately concepted."

"Conceived."

"Whatever! Now's not the best time to correct my grammar, Deuce. Just promise you won't miss the birth of your child."

"I'll be there. I promise. We've got time, right? You just said so!"

"Deuce, if you . . ."

"I'll bet you," I said, glancing toward the crowd. I could still see Susan, but she was about to round the corner toward the fairgrounds and I was going to lose her. "I'll bet you I'll be there."

"Bet me what? And are you wagering on the birth of your child?? Right now??"

"I make it there in time, I get to name the baby," I said. "I don't, you get full naming power."

She started to say something, but then thought about it. I think at that point she actually would've been glad for me to miss it.

"Full naming power?" she asked. "No arguments?"

"None. But if I get there, I get full naming rights."

Her voice was drowned out by the roar of a motorcycle behind us.

Butch had pulled up, his helmet on, his sunglasses on, a stern expression on his face.

And a massive flag with George's face on it mounted on the back of his bike.

"She's running!" he yelled. "You need a lift?"

"What?"

"The Blamunski woman," he said. "I heard part of your conversation. She's running. You need a lift before she gets away?"

I looked at Julianne.

"I swear to God, you better be there," she said. "Go."

I kissed her cheek. "I will be. Full naming rights."

I looked at Butch. "You got another bike that could get her to the hospital?"

Butch turned around, put his fingers to his lips, and ripped off an ear-piercing whistle. Two bikes immediately roared in behind him, both with the same George flag attached to the back of them.

"This woman needs a ride," Butch yelled. "Take her wherever she tells you!"

Julianne's forehead was in her hand.

I climbed on the back of Butch's bike and shoved on an extra helmet he'd handed me. "I love you! I'll be there!"

"I'm going to give your kid the worst name ever, Deuce Winters!" she yelled, shaking her head.

So I had some incentive to get to the hospital in time.

47

"You like the flags?" Butch called over his shoulder. "Told you it'd be good!"

My parents were near the judging platform when the chaos broke loose and my mother was already to the street by the time I realized I needed her. She assured me she had Carly and also assured me I would owe both her and my father an explanation when time allowed.

Butch and I were still snaking through the crowd on the street, the parade now at a complete standstill thanks to C.A.K.E.'s antics. I'd lost Susan while getting on the bike, but Butch said he had a bead on her and he was doing his darnedest to get us through the masses without flattening anyone.

I clutched the seat because I couldn't bring myself to put my arms around Butch. "Yeah! Awesome!"

He nodded and hit the throttle and we jerked forward into a small opening in the crowd. If anyone thought it was odd that we were trying to get through, they didn't show it. They were too caught up in the hosing down of the judges.

It took us several more minutes to get to the end of Main and I didn't see her anywhere. "Where'd she go?"

"Toward the arena," he said over his shoulder. "I saw her turn into the grounds."

I nodded. It was an odd choice if she was trying to hide. The fair was nearly empty—because everyone was at the parade—and she'd be easy to spot. But maybe her car was parked on the other side of the grounds in the main lot. Maybe she was trying to cut through the fairgrounds to get to her car.

Butch jumped the sidewalk and we hit the dirt path that led to the entrance. He turned the throttle again and we shot through the gates, dust clouds blossoming around us. I moved my hands from the seat to him, trading vanity and ego for safety.

We roared around the exhibit buildings, past the food stand, and toward the arena. The main gate to the arena was open and Butch punched the throttle again and we rocketed through the entrance into the massive dirt arena.

The entire grandstand was empty, except for Susan, who was sitting in the first row. She didn't run when she saw us, but she did look confused.

Which didn't make any sense to me. Why

had she tried to sneak away from the parade to go sit by herself in the stands?

Butch brought the bike to a halt near the steps to the grandstand, a final dust cloud swallowing us. I coughed and slid off the back.

"What's going on?" Susan demanded.

"Why are you running?" I asked, climbing over the railing to where she was sitting.

"Running? What are you talking about?"

"I saw you take off in the chaos at the parade," I said. "I didn't think you'd ever leave the 4-H float. You were running away after our conversation."

"What are you talking about?"

"You killed George, didn't you?"

"I told you, I had an alibi."

"But you didn't tell me what it is. So why are you running?"

Her face screwed up with agitation. "I wasn't running! I didn't kill anyone!"

Her conviction weakened mine. "But you left the parade."

"Because he told me to meet him here!" she bellowed.

"Who did?"

She pointed over my shoulder. "Butch!"

My stomach dropped and I turned around slowly.

Butch was resting against his motorcycle, aiming a gun at both of us.

48

"Butch, what the hell are you doing with a gun?" Susan asked.

"Taking care of loose ends," he said, smiling.

"Loose ends? What?" She looked at me. "What's he talking about?"

"I have no idea," I admitted.

Butch just smiled.

"He called me fifteen minutes ago and told me to leave the parade," Susan said. "He told me to meet him here and that it was an emergency."

"You two know one another?" I asked.

Susan's face flushed.

Butch grinned. "Oh, yeah. We absolutely do."

I was still in the dark.

"We, um, well," Susan stammered. "Butch and I . . ."

"I think the correct term is friends with benefits," Butch said. "We sleep together. Excuse me. We sleep together when she isn't pining for George."

"I wasn't pining for George."

Butch rolled his eyes, but kept the gun steady.

My stomach churned. "How long were you seeing each other?"

"A few months," Susan said. "We've been sorta off and on for a few months."

"More off than on," Butch said, shaking his head.

"Why the hell do you have a gun?" Susan demanded. "What is going on?"

"I think I have an idea," I said, my mind working everything over.

They both looked at me.

"Butch killed George," I said.

Susan gasped, but Butch stayed silent.

"No," Susan said. "That can't be true. You wouldn't do that. Butch?"

Butch didn't say anything.

"I was asking you about your alibi," I said to Susan. "Back at the float. Did Butch call you after that conversation?"

She blinked several times. "Well, yeah."

"Guess he overheard most of our conversation," I said, glancing at him.

Butch shrugged.

"But that doesn't make any sense," Susan cried. "Butch was my alibi. I was with him the night before you found George in the freezer."

"The entire night?"

She thought for a moment and then her face paled. "No."

Butch's mouth twitched at the corners.

"I broke up with him," Susan said quietly. "I told Butch that I didn't wanna see him anymore."

"Because you were still pining for George," Butch said, frowning.

"So we argued for most of the night," she continued. "He didn't want to break up. He wanted to keep seeing me. He was mad at me. But our relationship was . . . is . . . over. I thought I finally got that through to him. And then he finally left. It was early morning." She nodded slowly. "It was sunrise. It had taken me the entire night to get him to leave. He didn't want to go, but he finally did."

The pieces of the puzzle were sliding together.

I looked at Butch. "You really don't wanna make this worse for yourself."

"That's why I have the gun," he said, grinning. "I'm no dummy. I'm going to make it easier for myself. So you don't need to waste your breath and go all Law and Order on me."

"Was it an accident?" I asked, trying to buy myself some time to think about how to get out of this mess.

"I don't know what you're talking about," he said, raising his eyebrows. His smile said otherwise.

"You *really* killed George?" Susan asked, incredulous. "Sweet George?"

"Let's remember your sweet George was in love with sweet Matilda," Butch said, frowning.

"He was not in love with you, which you were too dumb to see."

"How did it happen?" I asked.

Butch was ignoring me, though, focused on Susan. "Your sweet George wanted nothing to do with you. He told you to take a hike."

"Stop," she said.

"He couldn't stand you," he continued. "He told you he didn't want anything to do with you."

I couldn't fault George there.

Susan bit her lip.

"But me?" he said, pointing his own finger at his chest. "Me? I've been there for you. Always trying to help you out. Do whatever you ask. And what thanks do I get?" He shook his head, disgusted. "You tell me we're done because you want to try again with George. Only George is already in love with someone else and has absolutely zero interest in trying anything again with you."

The pseudo-love triangle was making my head hurt. It seemed as if Susan had tried to replace George with Butch and, while that hadn't worked for her, he apparently had taken to the role.

Maybe a bit too much.

"I even went to check with him for you," he said, frowning like he smelled something rotten.

"You did what?" Susan asked.

"I went to make sure there was no chance he'd get together with you," he said, waving the gun at her. "You were all broken up that he'd told you to stop bothering him and, stupid me,

I thought I'd go tell him he'd hurt you and maybe that might change his mind. Even though you'd just told me we had no future. Because I'm *that nice.*"

The way he was waving the gun around and talking, Butch seemed anything but nice.

"So you went to tell him about Susan's feelings for him?" I asked, scanning the arena and the grandstand.

We were still alone. The parade must have stalled out completely and I imagined everyone in the town was trying to sort out the commotion.

"Yeah," he said, annoyed. "I left her house after she told me we were through and went right to his house. Woke his dumb butt up to tell him he was passing up a great opportunity with Susan."

"And what'd he say?"

"He told me to get off his property," Butch said, narrowing his eyes. "I thought that was rude."

"George was never rude," Susan said. "He didn't have it in him."

"Whatever," Butch said. "I didn't like the way he dismissed me. He wouldn't even listen to me. I mean, I was trying to do the guy a favor. So I wouldn't leave." He chuckled. "He didn't like that, either, but he couldn't do anything about it."

Butch seemed to enjoy his role as kind of a bully. I thought that joining a motorcycle club probably only empowered his sense of worth.

And if he really was that hung up on Susan, he seemed like he was more than capable of hurting someone.

"So he decided he was just gonna leave, since I wouldn't," Butch said. "So I followed him here to the fairgrounds."

"What did you do to him?" Susan said, her hands on her cheeks.

Butch chuckled. "Well, it was sort of an accident. He wouldn't listen to me. I tried to get him to listen to me. For *you*, Susan. I tried to talk to him for you."

Susan was crying now, tears running over her hands, which were plastered to her cheeks. For the first time, I felt a little sorry for her.

"I gave him a little shove," Butch said. "And he didn't really like that. And, then, when he took a swing at me, I shoved him a little harder."

Susan sobbed quietly, her cries echoing up the stairs of the grandstand, and I didn't say anything.

Butch shuffled his feet. "He sorta hit his head—on a brick—and didn't get up."

"He was dead?"

Butch hesitated, then nodded.

"So you just put him in the freezer?" I asked.

He hesitated, then nodded again. "Didn't really know what else to do with him."

"Call the police," I said. "Or an ambulance. Nine-one-one would cover all your bases. He took a swing at you. You could've claimed self-defense."

"Yeah, those didn't occur to me," he said, shrugging.

Clearly.

"And let's face it," Butch said. "I pushed him. I knew it would come out about me and Susan. I knew what it would look like. Putting him in the freezer seemed like the right thing to do."

That was something I never expected to hear anyone on the planet say.

"And you knew eventually I'd get to Susan," I said.

Butch chuckled again. "Well, I saw the opportunity to push you that way."

He certainly had and I'd let him do it. He'd subtly pointed me in her direction and I had strolled right down that path. I'd jumped to conclusions and assumptions and it had put me right at the end of a handgun.

Well done.

49

Butch moved Susan and me to the bottom of the grandstand at the far end of the arena, farther away from the gate, the gun still trained on us.

"So now what?" I asked.

"Good question," he said, rubbing his chin. "I can't just trust you to keep your mouths shut."

"Oh, I will!" Susan said. "I won't say anything!"

He rolled his eyes. "Right. That'll happen right about never."

"So then what?" I said.

I wanted to figure out what I was dealing with and also buy some more time. So far, I was getting the time, but nothing was coming into my head as to how to save Susan and myself. Butch may have killed George, but it did seem to be accidental to me. So maybe he wasn't ready to deliberately kill anyone.

"Well, I gotta figure out where to put your bodies," he said, his mouth twisted in thought.

Or, maybe he was.

Susan let out a loud whimper.

At the far end of the arena, I could see movement behind the fence, but I wasn't sure who or what it was. I tried not to look, because I didn't want Butch to turn around. He wasn't close enough for me to leap at him if his attention was diverted elsewhere. I needed to just keep him occupied.

"You think you can just shoot us and get rid of us and no one will know?" I asked. "Butch, the entire town saw me on the back of your bike at the parade. I mean, you spoke to my wife and arranged a ride for her. People aren't going to just forget that. It ties you directly to me."

He thought hard for a moment, temporarily stumped. Then a slow grin spread across his wide face. "I can make it look like Susan did it. Everyone also saw her leave. I tried to help, but she knew you were asking too many questions and, since *she* killed George, she figured she had to off you." His grin grew wider. "Then I found her with the gun, we struggled, and the gun went off." He snapped the fingers of the hand that wasn't holding the gun. "Bingo!"

I hated to say it, but that actually sounded like a decent plan. He could probably come up with someone who knew about Susan and

George, so he could make that connection. And people had seen me talking with Susan.

Butch was actually turning out to be smarter than I'd anticipated, and that was a problem. I really wanted to see my wife and daughter again, and my new child for the first time. I did not want to die at the fair.

There was more movement behind the fence. I tried not to look at it.

"People will hear the gunshots," I said. "And then you'll have to move our bodies. Gonna be tough to do when everyone starts pouring into the fairgrounds here soon."

His grin faded. He hadn't considered that and it was a roadblock in his grand plan.

The gate at the end of the arena started to move. Quietly.

"Look, if you go to the authorities now," I said, "you can tell them it was an accident. If you kill us, there's no going back. There's no way out. Don't make it worse for yourself, Butch."

"I appreciate the offer to help, Deuce," Butch said. "But I don't think your TV movie of the week logic is gonna work for all of us." He smiled. "I got a truck. I'll figure out a way to get your bodies out of here. I'm sure it'll work out."

Susan whimpered again.

"Your brothers in the Petal Dawgs know you killed George?" I asked, reaching for what I figured was the final straw.

Butch's face darkened. "No. They do not."

"I don't think they'd like the fact that you hurt one of your own," I said. "You told me something like that."

"Which is why they can't ever know," he said, the lines in his forehead thick and deep. "I'd be removed from the brotherhood. Forever."

The gate at the far end was almost open. I could see what was there.

Salvation.

But I needed to keep Butch occupied.

I slid in front of Susan, obscuring her view of the gate. I didn't want her to give anything away.

I pulled my cellphone out of my pocket. "Too late, Butch."

He looked at me, confused. "Too late? For what?"

"I've recorded all of this," I lied, holding up the phone. "Everything you've just said? I've got it."

His eyes locked onto me, processing my words. "Give me the phone."

"No," I said. "Let us go and I'll delete it. You can handle the murder how you want. Tell everyone it was an accident or something. But you've got to let us go."

"Not gonna happen."

I shrugged. "Okay. Your choice. I'm sending this now to several people." I made a show of tapping on the phone.

Butch hesitated, then started walking quickly in my direction. "Gimme the phone, Deuce."

"Too late, Butch," I said, shaking my head. "I'm sending it now. I gave you a chance."

He took several more steps toward me and leveled the gun at me. "Then it's too late for you."

And then a tidal wave hit.

50

Water streamed from one of the hoses inside the paper-mâché Earth, knocking Butch to the ground. Victor held the hose steady and Butch rolled farther away in the mud of the arena floor, the gun now lying in a massive puddle.

I leapt over the railing, splashed down in the mud puddle, and grabbed the soaking wet gun. The water stream shut off and I aimed the gun at a coughing and dripping Butch.

"You got him?" Victor yelled from inside the Earth.

"Got him."

He said something to the driver of the pickup and they pulled forward, toward us. The driver pulled around so that the Earth came up next to me.

"Cops are on their way," Victor said, laying the hose down.

"How'd you know?"

"I got your voice mail," he said. "Thanks for

waking me up, by the way. I was napping. I got to the parade and saw all the chaos. And your wife, on the back of a motorcycle."

I had a moment of panic, wondering if it was all some sort of elaborate setup and Julianne was in danger. But I quickly ruled that out. Butch had made it clear that he'd acted alone and no one knew what he'd done.

"She told me that you'd taken off toward the fairgrounds," he said. "I got over here and peeked through the fence. Saw you there and decided I liked you better alive than dead." He motioned at the truck. "They were coming through the grounds and I commandeered them."

"Commandeered?"

"Okay, I saw the kid driving the truck and a hose hanging over the back and paid him fifty bucks," he said. "By the way, you owe me fifty bucks."

"Noted."

"I'm assuming there's a good reason that dude was holding you at gunpoint?"

I quickly explained to him what had happened and what I'd learned from Butch's confession.

Victor shook his head. "Man, I was sure that old woman was the one. She fooled me."

I nodded. Butch had caught me by surprise. He'd never been on my list. Even though I hadn't known anything about his relationship with Susan, I'd overlooked him. That night at the board meeting, the way he'd gone after the board, I'd pegged him as a good guy, a guy who was on the same side as me.

Wrong.

Deuce Winters, failed detective.

I shielded my eyes from the blazing sun with my hand. "Can you handle this? I need to get to . . ."

"The hospital," Victor said. "Was wondering if you'd get around to remembering about that." He hopped down out of the truck and pointed at the driver. "You get this guy to the hospital and there's fifty more bucks in it for you. Interested?"

The driver grinned. "For sure."

Victor glanced at Butch, who was still on his back in the mud, a resigned expression on his wet, muddy face. Susan was sitting still on the bleachers, sobbing her eyes out. "Yeah, I can handle these two. Go."

"Thanks, Victor," I said, handing him the gun and climbing into the truck. "For everything."

"Yeah, yeah, yeah," he said, frowning. "I'm the best."

As the pickup roared out of the dirt arena, I wasn't about to tell him that he was, but I silently agreed.

51

Julianne did not look happy to see me. "Oh. You're here."

I sat down on the chair next to her hospital bed, exhausted, sweat dripping down my face. "I'm here."

She shifted on the bed. "Yes. You are."

"How are you?" I glanced anxiously at the IV taped to her hand and the monitors that beeped continuously.

She ignored my question. "You look . . . warm."

"It's hot out," I said. I closed my eyes. "Oh, and I was kidnapped."

"Kidnapped?"

"Well, not so much kidnapped as fooled."

"Fooled? You?" Julianne gripped the sides of the hospital bed. "That's hard to believe."

"Are you all right? Should I call for the nurse?"

She waved her hand in dismissal. "I'm fine.

Tell me what happened. Distract me, dammit, so my body won't explode."

I explained what had happened after she'd left.

She took a deep breath. "I'm glad I saw Victor, then."

"Me, too." I stared at her for a long moment. "I'm sorry."

"For what?"

"For leaving you," I said. "For letting you get here on the back of some motorcycle. For all of that."

She reached for my hand. "It's you being you."

"Well, maybe being me is a bit too much," I said, fanning myself with my hand. "I'm not sure I'm cut out for investigating anymore."

She smiled. "You'll change your mind."

"I'm serious, Jules," I said, shaking my head. "We're about to have a baby. I don't need to be doing this anymore. I'd rather be at home with the kids and help you with your practice and just be a dad and a husband."

She eyed me cautiously. "You get . . . restless."

"I know I do," I admitted. "So maybe you'll need to remind me of this moment."

She laughed softly. "I'll try, but I doubt it'll do anything."

"And in addition to being a crappy parent, I've also been a crappy dad. Speaking of which, where is our daughter?"

"Still with your parents," Julianne said. "They took her downstairs to the cafeteria to get something to eat. She said all of this waiting was making her hungry."

She paused and her face screwed up with concentration. She breathed deeply through her nose, and I knew a contraction was bowling her over. She expelled her breath slowly. "Your mom said they'd keep her down there until you told them it was okay to come back up."

"Okay," I said. "How are you?"

"I'm fine," she lied. "I feel better than you look, I think."

I was still having trouble catching my breath and I couldn't cool off. "I'm okay."

"You look pale," she said. "You need some water. I think the sun got to you."

"I'll get some," I said. "How close are you?"

She leaned back against the mountain of pillows behind her. "I don't know."

"What can I do?" I asked, feeling helpless. It was just like it had been with Carly. Julianne lying in a hospital bed, gritting her teeth and sweating, then screaming as she went into transition. As excited as I'd been about being so close to meeting our first child, I'd felt awful for putting her through that kind of pain.

On cue, she winced and squeezed my hand and I felt like the biggest jerk alive for getting her knocked up again. After a few seconds, she let go. "Soon. Kid's coming soon."

My head hurt and I felt a little dizzy. My throat was dry. But she wanted to be distracted. And we still had business to discuss.

"So. I made it here before the baby was born," I said.

Her expression returned to the one I'd seen when I first got there. "I realize that."

"You know what that means?"

"Yes." She sucked in a breath and squeezed her eyes shut. I glanced at the clock. Her contractions were less than three minutes apart. "I don't have to kill you."

I forged ahead with my distraction tactic. "It also means I get full naming rights."

She folded her arms across her chest and glared at me. "I just said that so you'd get here."

"We made a bet," I reminded her. "And I won. Fair and square."

"What if I don't like your choice?" she asked.

"You'll have to live with it," I said, wiping more sweat from my forehead. "Do you have water in here?"

"No," she said. "I'll buzz the nurse." She grabbed her little remote thing and pressed the button. "Now you owe me."

"Owe you?" I was feeling a little disoriented.

"For getting you water," she answered. "So I'd like naming rights back." A whimper tore through her and she writhed in the bed, twisting and bucking.

"Jules," I said, alarmed. But my voice sounded hollow and she looked like I was seeing her through a tunnel.

"I'm fine," she snapped, her voice warbling in my ringing ears. "Water for naming rights. Even trade."

The dizziness picked up and I felt like the chair beneath me was on roller skates. I closed my eyes for a second and the chair seemed to slide faster.

"Deuce?" I heard Julianne say. "Are you all right?"

I tried to open my eyes, but they wouldn't open. "Uh . . . I'm . . . dizzy."

"Hang on," she said. "The nurse should be here any second."

"Okay," I said, steadying myself with my hand against the bed. "Okay. And, yeah, names . . . ."

"Deuce?" Julianne said, but her voice sounded far away. "Are you going to faint?"

I was about to tell her no, but then I fainted.

52

"You fainted?" my father asked, then chuckled. "I forget. Were you the one having the baby?"

My parents were in the chairs next to the window in Julianne's hospital room. Carly was on one side of Julianne in the bed, I was on the other.

And Julianne was holding our brand new son.

"It was the heat," I said. "I was running around outside in the heat and didn't have enough to drink. Doctor said mild heat exhaustion."

"Oh, right," he said, making a face like he was impressed. "And you were fighting crime. Julianne, explain to me why you stay married to him again?"

Julianne smiled, but didn't take her eyes off our son. "Because I love him."

The nurse had arrived in the room as soon as I'd passed out. She'd hauled me into a chair and gotten me some ice and some juice. I came to just as Julianne was fully dilated. They tried to get me to sit and rest, but I refused. I sucked down two glasses of apple juice, crunched on the ice, and rinsed my face off with cold water before the doctor had arrived and ordered Julianne to push.

Once the baby decided he wanted out, he'd wasted no time. Five minutes later, our son arrived, red faced and howling, and Julianne and I both cried along with him. The tiredness and light-headedness were gone. I felt wide-awake and clearheaded. And ecstatic. Because I was no longer the only one with testosterone in my family.

"When's he going to open his eyes?" Carly asked for the third time, staring at the tiny bundle cradled in Julianne's arms.

"Soon," Julianne promised, tucking the blanket in around his tiny chin. Then she reached over and touched Carly's cheek. "Soon."

"Cops came and arrested that clown you rode off with," my dad said. "Think they might've detained Susan Blamunski, too."

I wondered how Butch would handle that. Would he confess outright like he did to me or would he try to find a way to worm his way out of it? Either way, I was sure I'd have to end up talking to the police.

"And, after the shenanigans at the parade, I think we'll be declining that company's offer to drill on our property," my dad continued. "I don't think it's worth it."

"A lot of money," I reminded him. "They'll pay you a lot of money."

He shrugged. "Eh. We got a little money. I don't think I want all those yahoos digging around and squirting water everywhere. Sometimes, money isn't worth it."

After everything I'd learned in the previous few days, I had to agree with him.

"I have a question," my mother said.

"What?" I asked, apprehensive.

"Do we have a name?" she asked. "He's an hour old and I know names were not discussed publicly prior to his birth, but I'd like to think you might name that little boy soon."

Julianne shifted in the bed and handed him to me. "Deuce is naming him."

I'd forgotten how light newborns were. I cradled him to my chest like a football. He gurgled, his mouth a perfect O. His eyes squeezed shut tighter and his nose twitched and he was perfect.

I looked at Julianne. "Really?"

"Deal's a deal," she said, smiling.

"Oh dear Lord," my father muttered. "This should be good."

"Let's name him Victor!" Carly said.

I laughed at that and looked down at my son. "Andrew, for Mom's dad."

My mother held a hand up to her mouth, pleased.

"Charles, for Julianne's dad," I said.

Julianne's eyes were misty.

"And Eldrick, for you, Dad," I said.

He looked surprised and, for once, had nothing to say. This may have been one of the greatest accomplishments of my life—causing him to go speechless.

I looked at my son. "Andrew Charles Eldrick Winters."

"I like it," Julianne whispered.

"And we'll call him by his initials," I said.

I could see all of them thinking, working the letters in their heads, coming to the same conclusion at about the same time.

"Ace," Julianne said, closing her eyes and shaking her head. But she was smiling.

"Oh good Lord," my father said, rolling his eyes. "I knew you'd do something goofy."

"I think it's cute," my mother said.

"I like it," said Carly, grinning at me.

"Me, too," I said. I looked at Julianne. "How about you?"

She opened her eyes, still smiling. "Ace and Deuce. I don't like it."

My heart sank. "No?"

"No," she said, but she was still smiling. "I love it."

1

"The King of Soccer is missing," Julianne said into my ear.

I was standing on the sideline, sweating, concentrating on the swarm of tiny girls chasing after a soccer ball. As the head coach of my daughter's soccer team, the Mighty, Fightin', Tiny Mermaids, it was my sworn duty to scream myself silly on Saturday afternoons, hoping they might play a little soccer rather than chase butterflies and roll around in the grass. As usual, I was failing.

I gave my wife a quick glance. "What?"

"The King of Soccer is missing," she repeated.

Before I could respond, my five-year-old daughter, Carly, sprinted toward me from the center of the field, ponytail and tiny cleats flying all around her.

"Daddy," she said, huffing and puffing. "How am I doing?"

I held my hand out for a high five. "Awesome, dude."

She nodded as if she already knew. "Good. Hey, are we almost done?"

"About ten more minutes."

She thought about that for a moment, shrugged, and said, "Oh. Okay." Then she turned and sprinted back to the mass of girls surrounding the ball.

Except for the ones holding hands and skipping around the mass of girls surrounding the ball.

I took a deep breath, swallowed the urge to yell something soccer-ish, and turned back to Julianne. "What?"

She was attempting to smother a smile and failing. "Sorry. Didn't mean to interrupt the strategy session, Coach."

"Whatever."

She put her hand on my arm. "I was trying to warn you. Moises Huber is missing."

Moises Huber, aka the King of Soccer, was the president of the Rose Petal Youth Soccer Association. He oversaw approximately two hundred teams across all age groups, close to two thousand kids, five hundred volunteers, and about a billion obnoxious parents.

He was also a bit of a jerk.

"Missing?"

"Hasn't been seen in three days, and Belinda wants to talk to you about it."

I shifted my attention back to the game. Carly broke free from the pack with the ball and loped toward the open goal. My heart jumped, and I moved down the sideline with her. "Go! Keep going!"

Several of the girls trailed behind her, laughing and giggling, not terribly concerned that they were about to be scored upon.

Carly approached the goal, settled the ball in front of herself, shuffled her feet, and took a mighty swing at the ball.

It glanced off the side of her foot and rolled wide of the goal and over the touchline.

My heart sank, and the gaggle of parents behind me in the bleachers groaned.

Carly turned in my direction, grinned, and gave me a thumbs-up. I smiled back at her through the pain and returned the thumbs-up.

She sprinted back toward her teammates.

Maybe we needed to practice a little more.

I walked back up the sideline to Julianne. "Why does she want to talk to me about it?"

"I think it has to do with you being a superb private eye and all," Julianne said.

"I'm not a private eye."

"Those fancy cards you and Victor hand out beg to differ, Coach."

After successfully proving my innocence in the murder of an old high school rival, I'd reluctantly joined forces with Victor Anthony Doolittle in his investigation business. On a very, very, very limited basis. We were still trying to figure out if we could coexist, and the jury was still deliberating.

I frowned. "What does *missing* mean? Like he's not here today?"

Julianne shrugged. "Dunno. But you can ask her yourself." She tilted her chin in the direction of the sideline. "She's coming your way, Coach." She kissed me on the cheek. "And don't forget. We have a date tonight."

"A date?" I asked.

"Well, a date sounds classier than using you for sex," she said, slipping her sunglasses over her eyes. "But call it what you like. Coach." She gave a small wave and walked away.

I started to say something about being objectified—and how I was in favor of it—but Belinda Stansfield's gargantuan body ate up the space Julianne had just vacated.

"Deuce," Belinda said in between huffs and puffs. "Need your help."

Her crimson cheeks were drenched in sweat, and her gray T-shirt was ringed with perspiration. Actually, it appeared as if all 350 pounds of Belinda were ringed in perspiration.

She ran a meaty hand over her wet forehead and smoothed her coarse brown hair away from her face. She took another huff—or maybe it was a puff—and set her hands on her expansive hips.

"Middle of a game here, Belinda," I said, moving my gaze back to the field, which I found far more pleasant. "Can't it wait?"

"No can do, Deuce," she said. "This is serious business."

Carly tackled one of the opposing girls, literally threw her arms around her and took her to the grass. They dissolved into a pile of laughter as the ball squirted by them.

"Um, so is this, Belinda."

"Oh, please, honey," she said, shading her eyes from the sun. "These little girls care more about what's in the cooler after the game than the score. And these parents don't know a goal from a goose. You are a babysitter with a whistle. Get over yourself."

Couldn't have put it better myself.

"What's up?" I asked.

"Moe's done and gone and disappeared."

"Like, from the fields?"

"Like, from Rose Petal."

Tara Little started crying and ran past me to her parents. We were now down a Fightin' Mermaid.

"Since when?"

"Today's Saturday," she said, swiping again at the sweat covering her face. "Last anyone saw him was Wednesday."

"Maybe he went on vacation," I said.

"Nope."

"Maybe he's taking a long nap."

"Deuce. I am not kidding."

The pimple-faced referee blew his whistle, and the girls ran faster than they'd run the entire game. They sprinted past me to the bleachers, where a cooler full of drinks and something made entirely of sugar awaited them. Serious soccer players, these little girls.

I took a deep breath, tired from yelling and baking in the sun, and adjusted the visor on my head. "Okay. So he's missing."

She nodded, oceans of sweat cascading down her chubby face. "And there's something else you should know."

I watched the girls, red-faced and exhausted, sitting next to each other on the metal bleachers, sucking down juice boxes, munching on cookies, and swinging their legs back and forth.

There were worse ways to spend a Saturday.

"What's that?" I asked.

"Seventy-three thousand bucks," Belinda said.

"What? What are you talking about?"

She shifted her enormous body from one tree stump of a leg to the other.

"Moe's missing," Belinda said. "And he took seventy-three thousand dollars with him."

2

"All the summer and fall registration fees," Belinda said. "Gone."

The girls were now chasing one another, the parents were chatting, and Belinda and I were sitting on the bottom of the bleachers.

"How is that possible?" I asked. "He just walked away with that much in cash?"

"The bank accounts are empty," she said. "They were full on Tuesday. Before he disappeared."

"Could be a coincidence."

"And I could be a ballerina," she said, raising an eyebrow. "It ain't a coincidence, Deuce."

No, it probably wasn't a coincidence. She was right about that.

"Don't you guys have some sort of control in place for that kind of thing?" I asked. "I mean, with the accounts. Multiple signatures or something like that?"

She shook her head. "Nope. Last year, when Moe was reelected, he demanded full oversight.

The board didn't like it, but he said he'd walk without it. So they gave it to him."

"Why did he want it?"

"No clue."

I spied Carly attaching herself to Julianne's leg. She was crying. Carly, not Julianne. Crying had become common after soccer games, the result of too much sugar and some physical exertion. It was less about being upset with something and more about it just being time to get home.

"I want to hire you, Deuce," she said. "We want to hire you. The board. To find him and the money. You and that little dwarf, or whatever he is."

A smile formed on my lips. I wished Victor was there to hear her description of him.

"I'll need to talk to Victor," I told her. "The little dwarf. To make sure he's okay with it."

"You two got so much work you're turning away business?"

As a matter of fact, we did. Or rather, Victor did. Since our initial escapade, people had been seeking us out left and right. My agreement with Victor allowed me the flexibility to work only when I wanted to. Fortunately, he'd been more than capable of handling most of the work and I'd been left alone to play Mr. Mom to Carly.

"No," I said, attempting to be diplomatic. "But we don't take anything on unless both of us agree."

She thought about that for a moment, then nodded.

Then her stomach growled.

"There's one more thing," she said.

"What's that?"

"We can't pay you."

I pinched the bridge of my nose. "That's gonna be a problem, Belinda. The little dwarf likes money. He tends not to work without it."

"I mean, we can't pay you up front," she clarified. "Everything we got, Moe took. You find him and the money, we'll pay you whatever we owe you."

I knew Victor was going to have a coronary over that.

"I'll talk to Victor and see what I can do," I said, standing.

She pushed her girth up off the bleachers, wobbled for a minute, then steadied herself. She wiped a massive hand across her wet brow.

"Well, I hope you can do something, Deuce," she said, a sour expression settling on her face. "Because that money? That's all we got. It doesn't come back, soccer don't come back."

"Really?"

"We are totally fee driven. Nothing in reserve. So unless you wanna foot the bill for uniforms and trophies and field space and insurance and who the heck knows what else, we need that money."

I glanced over at the remaining girls. Carly had detached herself from Julianne and was now playing some bastardized version of tag. Her team wasn't very good at soccer, but that didn't stop me from espousing the virtues of team sports at a young age. They weren't winning games, but I believed they were getting something out of playing.

"Why would he take the money, Belinda?" I asked.

"I got no idea," she said, shaking her head. "I really don't, Deuce. But we gotta have the money back. Now him?" She waved a hand in the air. "I couldn't care less whether that weasel comes back."

"Weasel?"

Her eyes narrowed. "You don't know him all that well, do you?"

I shrugged. I knew him from around town and from soccer meetings. A little pompous, but other than that, I didn't think much at all about him.

"No," I admitted. "I guess not."

"Weasel," she said. "Pure weasel."

"Why's that?"

"Because that's the way the good Lord made him," she said, frowning. "Or Satan. Whichever."

"So you aren't surprised he took the money, then?" I asked.

"I'm a little surprised," she said. "Because I didn't think even he'd pull something like this. But you know what's more surprising?"

I looked past her. Julianne now had Carly

in her arms and was waving at me. I was ready to go home and be objectified.

"Uh, no. What's more surprising?"

She hiked up her ill-fitting shorts and looked me dead in the eye.

"That no one's killed that weasel yet."

3

"You're kidding, right?" I asked as I loaded the soccer gear into the back of the minivan. Julianne and Carly were already settled in their seats. "Why would anyone want to kill Huber?"

"I'm just sayin'," Belinda said in between huffs and puffs, "he's not the most liked fella around Rose Petal."

"A lotta people aren't the most liked, Belinda. That doesn't mean they have a hit out on them."

She shaded her eyes from the sun, a drop of sweat hanging from the tip of her nose. "Lotsa reasons. A biggie?" She leaned closer to me, and I tried not to shrink away. "He cheats at poker."

"What?"

"Poker. He cheats."

I closed the back of the minivan. "What are you talking about?"

"Don't you play in one of them games? Where

all you daddies get together and pretend to be manly and play poker?"

I did, in fact. Last Friday of every month. A tight group of friends, we rotated homes and played until the wee hours of the morning, drinking beer, making fun of one another, and taking each other's money. It was less about the poker and more about the need to do some serious male bonding. Kind of like the kids and their soccer, but with more cursing and beer.

"Well, he used to play in a regular game," Belinda said, "but they found out he was cheating. Kicked his butt out."

"If it was anything like my game, you're expected to cheat."

She shook her head. "No. This was different. They played for stakes bigger than your daughter's lunch money." She nodded, as if confirming to herself what she was saying was true. "Ask around. You'll find out."

I knew that was true. Rose Petal wasn't big, and nearly everyone knew something about someone else's business. It was a fishbowl of sorts. And I had to admit as she was telling me this, I was surprised that I hadn't heard some version of Huber's cheating already.

"I'll get back to you, Belinda," I said, pulling the keys out of my pocket. "No promises, though. I have to talk to Victor first."

"I'll sit on him," she said.

"Huh?"

"I'll sit on that little man if that's what it takes to get him to agree," she said.

"I'll pass that along."

Belinda waddled away across the now empty parking lot, as everyone else had packed up and gone home. I slid into the driver's seat, shoved the key into the ignition, and fired up the air-conditioning.

"She is a large woman," Julianne said.

"And then some."

"She wants you to look for the King?"

"Yes."

"And you said?"

"That I had to talk with Victor first."

I backed out of the stall and headed out of the lot. I glanced in the rearview mirror. Carly was red-faced, and her eyes were glazed over. She was exhausted. Which meant a nap was on the horizon. Which meant . . .

"We may get some alone time," Julianne whispered.

"Was just thinking the same thing."

"You sure you aren't too tired, Coach?" She moved her hand and rested it on my thigh.

I smiled. "I'm so irresistible, aren't I?"

She lifted her hand. "I just need you to make the next baby. You're a conduit."

I glanced at her, and she wore the smirk she always wore that put me in my place.

We were ready for another child. We'd relished the first five years alone with Carly, and we'd done that on purpose. She was our first, and we wanted to dote on her, give her as much attention as possible. And we wanted to be rested before the second one came along.

Not that Carly was a tough kid—she wasn't—but any child will wear you out as he or she goes from infancy to toddlerhood to kindergarten.

People looked at us a little strangely. In Rose Petal you were expected to follow one kid with another, and then maybe another, so that your house was filled with small people all under the age of five. But Julianne and I had stood our ground against the peer pressure and had stuck to our plan.

However, it was time to enact phase two of our plan. Which, you know, I was kinda looking forward to. I wasn't going to mind if it took a while. Practice makes perfect.

I pointed the minivan in the direction of our home and tried to obey the speed limit. This was a hard thing to do, particularly when I saw Carly nod off in her car seat.

"She's out," I whispered.

"I know," Julianne whispered back. Her smirk morphed into a smile, and my foot slammed harder on the accelerator.

I slowed down enough so as not to cause the van to go airborne as we pulled into the driveway, and eased it into the garage. I kept the engine running until the garage door was down behind us, then shut off the ignition. Carly wasn't exactly a light sleeper, but she didn't need a lot of encouragement to wake up, either.

"I'll run her upstairs," I said.

"I'll be in the living room."

"The living room?"

The smile grew devilish. "We can be a little . . . noisier in the living room."

Oh, my. "I'll meet you there."

I managed to open the van doors, remove Carly from her seat, and get her into my arms without her stirring. I gave Julianne a thumbs-up, turned, and walked as quickly as I could into the house, up the stairs, and into her room. I laid her down on her bed and she squirmed a little, settling onto the blankets, but kept her eyes shut, smacking her lips.

I paused and smiled. It would be nice to have another of those. I liked being a dad. Even better, I loved being a dad who got to stay home with Carly, far more than I ever anticipated I would. Everyone had warned me that adding a second child to the mix might change my mind, but I was willing to take that chance.

If only because phase two sounded like so much fun.

I bounded down the stairs, careful to keep my footsteps light. I kicked off my sneakers, tossed my socks on top, and found Julianne stretched out on the sofa.

In black lingerie.

"Whoa," I said.

The devilish smile returned. "Such a way with words."

"Whoa," I said again.

"Good thing I don't need to be wooed."

"I could try and woo you."

"Come closer and whisper your woos in my ear."

I leaned down and stretched out my body on top of hers, every synapse in me firing like pistons in a race car. I felt sorry for those men who got bored with their wives. Julianne was more attractive now than the day I met her, and every time she smiled at me, butterflies still took off in my stomach.

She wrapped her arms around my neck and kissed me, setting off fireworks inside my head. Our bodies meshed together, and I realized there was no possible way phase two could ever be overrated.

"Don't you two have a bedroom?" a voice said from the entryway.

Julianne's body stiffened beneath me, and the fireworks in my head disappeared, replaced by a gathering fury that could be brought on by just one person.

"Don't stop on my account," the voice said. "I'll wait till you're done."

"What is he doing in here?" Julianne whispered, shrinking beneath me.

"I have no idea," I said, resting my forehead against hers. "Do we have to stop?"

"Deuce!" Julianne said in my ear. "Do something!"

I sighed and swiveled my head in the direction of the other, unwelcome voice.

Victor Anthony Doolittle waved his tiny fingers at me.

Friggin' midget.